MW01484174

THINGS I ALWAYS WANTED

KELSEY HUMPHREYS

PREFACE
SADIE CANTON

My hands shake a bit as I fumble with the little wooden box on my way down the ladder, either from the excitement or the cold - or the shock at finding such a precious box stuffed between macaroni noodle Christmas ornaments and a set of snow skis disintegrated to the point of becoming one with Dad's wooden attic floor.

I hustle inside to the guest bedroom to warm up. I can't believe I sat and sorted through that little box for over an hour. Okay, I can totally believe it. I'm getting sucked in, like I always do. I'm teetering on the edge, one minute away from opening my laptop and typing like a madwoman until I turn into a smelly garbage troll at my desk.

Just two months ago, just a few thousands words from finishing the last book in my Bolt Brothers series, I found the start of a dread lock in the hair at my base of my topknot-turned-scary-nest. It had formed around a blonde bobby-pin, which was particularly disturbing since I only ever buy brown hair pins.

I should take a break.

Still, the idea is filling me up now. It's grabbed my heart, it's taking over my brain and soon it will itch to come out through my fingers.

I set the box down on the dresser as if it's made of glass. I pace the room, wondering. Is this a good idea? A terrible idea? Is it inappropriate? Or totally fitting? I sigh and pull out my phone. Time to ask the advisory board, also known as my four beloved sisters. I spill the contents of the box on the dresser and take a photo.

Me: So... look what I found

[photo]

Susan: Are those mom and dad's?!?!?!

Sally: Mom and dad's what? What am I looking at?

Sam: OMG OMG OMG [heart eyes emoji] [heart eyes emoji]

Skye: Uh oh, Sam, you better find yourself a paper bag.

Me: These are mom and dad's old postcards and love letters

Susan: I'm getting choked up just looking at his pic, have you read them??

Me: A few

Sam: I want to read every single one!

Sally: Ew, what if there's sex stuff

Susan: It was the early eighties, I guarantee they didn't write about sex!

Skye: I just want to read mom's words

Susan: yeah same

Sally: okay same

Sam: [crying emoji] [crying emoji] [crying emoji]

Me: So, I have an idea...

Susan: ???

Skye: I know where this is going

Sam: Whatever it is, I love it already!!

Sally: ??

Me: How would you guys feel if I wrote their story? It's such a great story, it can just be for us, I don't even have to publish it.

Sam: YASSSSSS SADIE DO IT

Sam: I am having ALL THE FEELS!!!

Skye: I have mixed feels

Sally: Aw, I love their story

Susan: What will dad say?

Skye: Dad will say he's fine with whatever we want.

Me: True, so, what do we want?

Susan: I don't know

Skye: Let me guess, you already have the whole thing outlined in your head and are having to force yourself not to sit down and start writing right this second?

Me: True again, You know me well.

Sam: Please please please

Sam: Their story is so great, you have to!

Sam: Stop texting, start writing!

Skye: It IS a really great story...

Me: Also true!

Susan: Well if you're inspired, write it and then we can go from there

Sally: I'm grossed out that you're going to write about our parents making out

Me: LOL it won't actually be them in my head, and since it'll be set in the present, instead of the 80s, I think it'll be different enough.

Skye: I'm with Sally a little bit. Awkward feels.

Me: Yeah, ok. It might get weird. If it does I'll have Lorelai do the steamy scenes

Sam: OMG you and your bestie finally co-writing something!?

Sam: This just keeps getting better and better

Susan: I think I agree! I'm getting excited!

Me: So, Skye? Sal? Canton Advisory Board agrees?

Sam: Agree!

Susan: Agree

Sally: Agree

Skye: Agree

Skye: See you in a few weeks when you emerge from your writing black hole

Me: LOL Author Ogre Mode: Initiated

Susan: Please just remember to take breaks to eat and shower

Sally: [nose emoji]

Sam: GET OFF YOUR PHONE NOW!

Me: Okay going! Will eat! Will shower! Thank you guys for letting me try this.

Me: Love you, Bye

I sit down at my laptop with a smile. I take a deep breath and ready myself.

Time to dig deep into the beautiful, brilliant mind of my mother ...

PROLOGUE

THREE YEARS FROM NOW

My shock in this moment is illogical.

Years ago, I analyzed the data sets—our friendship, our emails, my emotional turmoil, Jonny's lack thereof—and there was only one logical conclusion to be found. It arrived in my consciousness suddenly, during what I dramatically named my Summer of Anguish. Dramatics are to be expected of a seventeen-year-old girl.

Lonely in California, I discovered the collected works of Nicholas Sparks. I studied all of his movies before speed-reading his novels. *The Notebook*, specifically, disrupted my emotions so much that my body produced tears. Tears over a fictional story.

I suppose it was not fictional to my subconscious.

There was a particular scene that inspired the hypothesis that has now been proven correct. In *The Notebook*, there is a scene in a restaurant when Lon proposes to Allie and immediately, even as she nods *yes,* her mind flashes back to Noah, her childhood boyfriend. I saw myself in Rachel McAdams' character—even if I didn't know how to properly apply lipstick or twirl in a dress. I would also never proclaim that I was a bird, or any other species, while running through the ocean.

But we weren't Allie and Noah.

Or, rather, I was an Allie without a Noah.

Because Noah loved Allie back.

I sat up on the couch in my brand new dorm room in a moment of scientific clarity.

I was irrationally in love with Jonny Canton.

And that love was going to ruin my life.

Now, here I am, my legs itching from contact dermatitis due to the dust on the engineered wood floor.

It would have been prudent to change my phone number.

Perhaps I should have moved away again.

As I stare at the phone in my hand, pixels blurring in my vision, I know.

I should not be surprised. Yet I am.

Because I never expected or imagined *this*.

CHAPTER 1

NOW

Tornado sirens. I hear them right now, nearby. They make my palms perspire and my heart beat irregularly every single time. It's odd. I was glad to be rid of their piercing clang the last four years, but I missed them as well.

They started it all.

Rotated my entire life 180 degrees.

The sound waves of those sirens helped shape me into the person I am today, metaphorically, of course.

Obviously, I'm grateful for the technology in a big-picture, full-scope, *saving the lives of everyone in America's heartland* kind of way. But it's also the sirens I blame. Not the tornado, which, if I remember correctly—as I always do—touched down for a total of forty seconds over five miles away.

Right now, it's a sunny Saturday at twelve o'clock sharp, and the state is testing the mechanism, as they have every Saturday since my family moved here. But the sirens weren't running a test on that hot, humid Tuesday afternoon.

I was brand new to Tulsa, Oklahoma, so I had no frame of reference to process what I was hearing. I stopped on my bike, frozen on the perfectly manicured neighborhood street, unsure of what was happening and wanting to examine the possibilities.

Before my brain had time to make sense of the strange noise, there he was. He was so tall and so old in my mind, even though he was just ten. Ten was pretty remarkable when you yourself were only seven.

His appearance was jarring back then like it is now. As an adult he has blonder hair and a larger frame, naturally, but the same green-blue stare. I didn't notice the other boys; I just saw him and those eyes. They had a sparkle that conjured an association with the sea my family had just moved away from. The group of smelly boys barreled past on bikes, scooters, and skateboards, headed to a house. But he stopped.

"You just moved here, right?" He asked me. I nodded. "That's the tornado sirens. You gotta get in a storm shelter or you'll probably die. Tornadoes kill people. Flatten a whole street. So. Yeah. Does your house have a shelter?"

I shook my head. I didn't actually know if our house had one, but it seemed pretty impressive to have one's very own survival bunker. That was surely something my father would've remarked on with pride when we moved in.

"Well," he motioned with his head toward his house, "you want to get in mine with us?"

I thought about it. Technically he was a stranger, but his house was only a couple lots down from mine. His facial features were open and eager, and he'd stopped for me. He seemed pretty smart, too, knowing all that information about tornadoes.

Also I didn't want to die, especially not by street flattening.

"O-k-k-kay."

One small, poorly partitioned word, and that was it.

That was the day I became best friends with Jonny Canton. Not that I had much of a choice in the matter. He was arresting, even then. He talked and laughed so easily with everyone, no one could resist him. I preferred to listen, as I was painfully shy and had significant trouble getting thoughts from what I learned was the Wernicke's Area of my brain out through my mouth. This difficulty was manifested as a stutter. Taking all of this into account, it was like Jonny was created in a lab with the specific objective of Sandra Friend Creation.

That was the first of a few grand summers together. Both of us were the youngest in our family, with older brothers who didn't care or notice what we were up to and parents who worked long hours.

We saw each other at school, but since he was three years ahead of me, we were never on the same schedule. He'd wave in the hall or thump me on the shoulder at the bus stop, but school time was filled with his very mature and sophisticated fifth-grade life.

The summers, however, they were ours. We ran all over our neighborhood like we were president of the Home Owners' Association. I always brought a backpack filled with snacks and, of course, multiple books. But I didn't accomplish much reading around Jonny. We were too busy biking, fishing, swimming, and sometimes playing with other kids.

And talking.

Boy howdy, as he would say, could Jonny talk back then. Mostly about turtles. He was mildly obsessed. Frogs, snakes, and other reptiles sometimes made their way into our conversation, but turtles (and tortoises and terrapins!) held his fascination the longest. I could understand his passion but felt it was misplaced. There are over nine hundred thousand species of bugs on this earth, a much more interesting field of study, in my seven-year-old opinion.

I remember during the first week of our friendship, he stopped rambling long enough to inquire, "You don't talk much, huh?"

I shrugged.

"That's okay, Sandy, you don't have to talk with me."

I remember how I exhaled with deep, introverted relief. And I smiled. No one had ever called me Sandy before. My big brothers called me Squirt, which I loathed. My parents were formal and serious to a fault, so I was only ever Sandra to them. I hadn't yet made any close friends in my short life. It was difficult to make friends when you did not verbally communicate.

I wondered occasionally why he stuck to me like an adhesive when he could have been riding around with other boys or even other kids his age. But Jonny was almost as "quirky"—my brother's description—as me, in his own way. He was never alone or settled. Even when he was quiet, he hummed or whistled. He had more energy than a thunderstorm, and it all seemed to release through his mouth. I think the other kids grew tired of listening to him.

I never did.

It was the following summer that I actually started responding. My parents befriended other parents on the street, and we began attending barbecues and pool parties. At one of those first few gatherings, I noticed how Jonny's older brother, Rob, teased him incessantly. The next day I set the record straight as we drank Capri Suns on the blistering concrete.

"H-hey, Jonny?"

"Yeah?" I never began our conversations, so he looked at me with as much shock and interest as he'd give a newfound baby box turtle. Those big teal eyes of his grew wide. I braced myself to spit out the sentence I had been practicing.

"I th-think your brother is a big t-t-t-turd, and I think you're really nice and f-funny and smart."

He looked away immediately and swallowed. He blinked hard, and I worried I'd said the wrong thing, so I quickly attempted a joke. "I mean, n-n-not as smart as me, of c-course."

He smiled. "No one is as smart as you, Sandy."

"I d-d-don't know, I didn't even know the difference between a t-tortoise and a t-t-terrapin before I met you."

He looked back at me. "Really? It's not in any of your big ol' chapter books?" I shook my head at his earnest face. "Cool," he said, then he got up and jumped into the pool. I followed after him, as always.

The sirens end their scheduled drill, and I survey the entirety of my closet, now strewn across my room in an unorganized way that makes me twitchy. If only I had had more classically feminine influences growing up, perhaps I wouldn't be so hopeless now.

It was our second summer when it was Jonny's turn to comfort me about said hopelessness. His brother bullied him, but that was inconsequential in comparison to my own bullies. Young girls are, unequivocally, the absolute worst. Especially when they are not yet skilled at hiding who and what they're whispering and giggling about.

I did everything in my power to blend into walls, to stay under everyone's radar, but teachers tended to drag me out into the spotlight. I hid my stutter well by staying as silent as possible at all times, unless asked a mathematical or scientific question. But that didn't stop my teachers from noting I'd aced a surprise science quiz everyone else had failed. It didn't keep the other girls from noticing I'd finished reading an entire book in two days. Or that I was given special math assignments because my brain was calculating three years ahead of schedule.

It happened over and over.

Jonny caught me crying on the bench by the neighborhood pond.

"What's wrong?" he said, sitting down next to me. I just shook my head and wiped my tears. He picked up a stone and tossed it so that it planed along the surface, skipping six times before sinking. It sunk, and he turned his attention back to me. "I think everyone wants to be the smartest. But they can't, because that's you. You already got that spot in your class, really, even in our neighborhood, Sandy. Even with kids older than you, like me. Sooo I think people who are mean to you, I think they want to be you."

I sniffed, unsure. "You think p-p-people want to...b-be like me?"

"Yup, and they can't. Not even close. So it makes them mad."

"Hm," I said, starting to feel better.

"So when people whisper and stuff, it's not that they don't like you. They're just mad." I nodded and smiled. "And if you think about it, that's kinda dumb...which doesn't help when what they want is to be smart!" He laughed hard at his own joke, and I laughed, too. He made it sound so simple.

I've never forgotten that conversation.

No one could ever cheer me up quite like Jonny.

I flop onto my clothing options with a sigh.

It's *Jon* now.

I try to shake the thoughts from my head as I stare at the ceiling.

What does it matter if he goes by Jon now?

I'm not Sandy anymore, either. I am a Stanford graduate at twenty! Magna Cum Laude, too! And, I remind myself as I look in the mirror, I finally have breasts. Not as impressive or important, but definitely noteworthy. Especially today. Mom repeatedly told me I'd be a late bloomer, but I held out very little hope. Still, there they are, at last.

All in all, I'm ready for tonight...aren't I? I'm smart, fun, funny... Admittedly the last two are rare, but they do happen when I'm comfortable with someone. Lee says I am hysterical. Plus, I'm a grown adult now. So why do I feel so painfully tense?

Perhaps I have miscalculated all of this. There will be so many people attending tonight, I'll be overwhelmed. Even if Jonny puts me at ease, I want to explain myself to him so badly, to make my case, that I'll likely revert to my bumbling, stuttering, shrinking self.

I shouldn't go. I should ask to meet up with him elsewhere, tomorrow. As if sensing my thoughts, my phone lights up.

"How did you know I was thinking of you precisely this second?" I ask my friend as I open up FaceTime.

"Ummm, because tonight is the big night, and I know you're lying on your bed, wondering how you can get out of going, wallowing in outfit choices, even though you have approximately seven more hours to get ready."

"Lee, are you some kind of sorceress? Because this is uncanny." I stand and flip the camera around to show her my bed covered in an explosion of fabrics.

"No, I just know my bestie." She takes a bite of Cinnamon Toast Crunch before continuing. I assume that's what I am hearing, because Lee Chang is always eating, and nine times out of ten she's eating cereal. "So, remind me again. You said Canton fireworks show. Is this like an intimate thing at their house?"

I laugh at the notion. "No, this is his dad's way of displaying his success to our whole community of friends. The event gets bigger every year. Last year I estimated there were over two hundred people."

"At their house?!"

"The country club."

Lee makes a disgusting gagging sound and an almost equally disturbing facial expression.

I laugh again. "Yes, it is a little unsettling. It is also *a lot* of people. My family and his family will be there along with everyone I grew up with, acquaintances from school, church...ugh."

"So, big party means in and out." She crunches again. "Just make an appearance."

"I suppose..."

"You cannot back out! You're going! When was the last time you saw him?"

"A year and a half. I didn't come home last summer, and his family was gone over the holidays last year. I saw him the Christmas before that."

"Read me his email again."

I reluctantly minimize her face and pull up my mail app, also known as the *window to the soul* of my relationship with Jonny. It feels uncomfortable to read an email to her. They are just words on a screen, but when sent from this sender, they're almost sacred to me now.

Sometime during our third summer, things with Jonny shifted. He was thirteen, and I was only ten, making the age gap between us absolutely gigantic. Other boys from the neighborhood joined us in our activities, which had transitioned to mostly swimming and video games in the air conditioning. But Jonny always invited me to join them. If he wasn't at the pool, I'd let myself into his house, and he would wordlessly hand me a game controller or pull up a chair.

One day Brock whined about me during a session of intense *Guitar Hero* in Jonny's basement game room.

"Why does your little sister always have to do everything with us?" he'd said.

"Because she does," Jonny replied. Then he popped him hard in the shoulder, and that was that. At the time, I'd thought it was so wonderful he'd claimed me as his sister.

I would relive that moment again and again throughout my life.

During the societal torture chamber that was middle school, Jonny found comfort with me. At least I think that's how I'd explain it now, looking back. While he and his pimply friends went through varying phases of awkward metamorphosis, I stayed the same. I listened to all of Jonny's insights about junior varsity and then varsity football, and when he started to go through spurts of quiet brooding, induced by his merciless older brother, I entertained him with science experiments, book summaries, and useless trivia.

Things shifted between us again when Jonny started high school. I didn't see him in the halls of the middle school anymore or get to ask him about his homework on the walk home from the bus stop. But beyond that, he closed off a part of himself, as if his new freshman world was too vast and incomprehensible for little seventh-grade me.

But then, thankfully, came email, during our fifth summer.

Jonny went away to summer camp for a whole month, as was his family tradition. He was nervous, and I was sad to lose my counterpart. Campers were allowed to send and receive email every day, so we set up email accounts to maintain contact. His smelly tween male friends were not going to email back and forth with him every day, so finally Jonny and I got back to a friendship that was singularly ours.

I remember how grown up it felt to have an email account at the age of twelve. I also remember the thrill when I'd hear the email notification on the ancient iPad I was allowed to use. And I heard the wondrous noise every day.

The emails were fun and easy, and they were ours. Even though the frequency has fluctuated over the years, the letters have remained. Well, "letters" is an exaggeration.

The last few years, I've kept up my emails, but Jonny started sending selfies in reply. He poses for me in fun spots in whatever city across the world that Canton Cards has taken him and his brother. Sometimes he writes a few words with his funny photos, but often he doesn't. Still, we've never ignored each other's almost-weekly messages.

For eight years.

I clear my throat and explain our latest messages to Lee. "So *my* email said I my lease was finally up and I was headed here, home, this week. "

"And how much you were going to miss your roommate and bestie so far away." Lee crunches.

"Obviously."

"K, and he said?"

"His email reads:

"So the prodigal brainiac returns! That means I'll see you at the annual Canton Family Fireworks extravaganza, right? RIGHT?

"That second right was in all caps. And the attached photo is a selfie of him with a sparkler that he sent me from the show last year."

Lee swallows loudly as she thinks. "So, it's officially go time. You tell him you are all grown up and you love him and want to have his babies."

"What! Absolutely not! I'm only twenty!"

She laughs loudly. "I didn't mean right now tonight. Do you even know how babies are made, little Sandy?"

"Lee. You know I'm not a virgin."

"So you've said." She draws the words out to tease me.

"Can we refocus, please?"

She laughs again. "Okay, geez. You tell me, what's your plan?"

I take a deep, shaky breath.

"The plan is that I tell him we should date. It is the natural progression of our friendship as adults. He hasn't seen me in eighteen months. I'm no longer a little kid following him around. Either he'll see that, or..."

"Or what?"

"Or I let it go." I sigh out of my lips, making a loud, spitty raspberry. "I ffffinally let him go." The sentence feels heavy and final on my tongue.

My friend feels the weight with me. "All right. Wow. Have you talked to Avery about what you're going to wear yet?"

"No, she hasn't gotten her wifi set up, much to my despair."

While every bit as smart, introverted, and driven as Lee and me, Avery Winston is, well, our *fun one.* The friend who makes you take study breaks and listen to abhorrent music and watch whatever unrealistic television show is currently trending.

"Oh, that's right. Well, show me and we'll figure it out."

"K."

I talk Lee through a few outfits laid across my bed.

She grunts. "Uh, yeah. We need Avery."

"Ughhhh!" I flop on top of my clothes. "Remember, this is a Fourth of July party in a hundred and five degrees and high humidity. Can I really wear anything other than a tank top and shorts?"

"No, I think not. Maybe just go with your tightest tank and your shortest shorts? That's what Avery would say, right?"

"Right." I set the phone down to change, and she starts talking to her view of my old room's oddly textured ceiling.

"So, are you suuuuure he isn't also secretly in love with you, too?"

"Positive."

"I mean, Sand, I love you, but you're not exactly perceptive to social cues. What if he's tried to make a move in the past and you just weren't pickin' up what he was puttin' down?"

I huff at her. "Because I've closely, painfully observed him with girls that he likes. There is a specific way he looks at them and talks to them or about them. He's never interacted that way with me."

"No long hugs or lingering stares where you thought he may kiss you?"

"Not once. I've always been firmly sorted in the little best friend category, bordering on the east with the little sister category. Ugh."

She ponders this. "Why east?"

"I don't know, I was just rambling nonsense because of nerves. Help me!"

"Right. Sorry. Tonight we get you out of that category. How will you explain everything to him?"

"With words, w-w-which is..." I take a deep, clarifying breath. "Which is why I'm calling you!" I almost yell it.

"Damn, all right, woman! Crap! I've never seen you like this."

"Sorry."

I sigh. It's true, I'm never like this. Nervous, shy, sputtering, and awkward, sure. But agitated to the point of raising my voice? Never. Unless Jonny Canton is involved.

"It's okay. Let's start our plan with the outfit. How's it looking?" I pick the phone back up and show her my reflection in my closet door mirror. I'm wearing a plain, tight, red tank and cut-off shorts. She doesn't say anything.

I let out an exasperated laugh. "So, that bad, huh?"

"I mean you look good, but not *I'm secretly in love with you please take me home and do me* good."

"Lee! Take me home and d-d-do me?!"

"Oh, I'm sorry are we not trying to move you from little child-hood friend category to hottie boss-ass bombshell category?" she asks sarcastically.

I sigh heavily. "You're right. Continue."

She straightens up, which I know means she's decided to invest in the experiment that is the reunion with my lifelong child-hood crush.

"Logic would say more skin. Those shorts are cute, but let's cut the frays so they're shorter. It is one hundred and five there, after all, which is absurd. Why would anyone live in such a place?"

I wince. "Cutting my own shorts? That sounds potentially disastrous."

"Watch a how-to on TikTok. You're going to be cutting open people's bodies and putting their bones back together, I think you can handle denim, Doctor."

"Touche, Doctor." I get to work on the shorts with an old pair of scissors while she talks.

"The next logical step would be breasts. Sad that you don't really have much cleavage. Do you own a push-up bra?"

"Maybe? I think I have one."

She nods back at me. "Good, go get it."

I dig and find a push-up bra that I haven't worn in years. It still fits on the last clasp, but since I've sprouted actual breasts, the little cups can barely contain me.

This thrills me.

"I do have a black tank top that's cut lower, but it's not very festive for the Fourth of July."

"Festive? Again, our objective is to move categories here! The color of your top is secondary!"

I laugh back at her. "You are doing a surprisingly good job of channeling your inner Avery right now. You objectivity has made you the teacher, and I am but a lowly pupil."

"I don't think you should say things like 'but a lowly pupil' tonight."

"But I wwwill, and you know it." We both cringe together. Then I pick up my phone and finally look in the mirror. "Well? How is this?" I immediately start shaking my head.

"WINNER!" She cheers.

"Lee, no, this does not fit properly. I look like a daytime television prostitute!"

"Categories, Sandra. Cat-e-gor-ies."

I nod as I laugh and cringe and tug at all the fabrics.

"And Sand," Lee continues, "if he doesn't get the message, if he doesn't see you in all your non-platonic, grown-up glory, he's not the one after all. I mean, babe, it's been your whole lives. Maybe it's time *he* moves categories? Maybe he get started as the old friend you lose touch with, ya know?" The thought causes physical pain in my head and stomach. She doesn't notice. "And, like we've discussed at length, you do not need a man at all. But strange, sappy, hopeless romantic that you are—and that's just for a normal person, not even a champion of science—consider this: how is your heart ever going to open up so *the one* can get in there?"

I scoff and gesture wide with my arm. "It is not as though I've ever had a line of men hopeful for the position."

"But you will, Dr. Sandra Hayes, you will."

"Ehh. We'll see."

I hear the pour of more cereal. "Text me every detail later?"

"I will. Bye."

"Bye!"

My stomach pulls tight and makes a peculiar set of noises. Only six-and-a-half hours to go.

CHAPTER 2

Time is so peculiar. When I'm trying to finish a chemistry final, it zooms by at 670 million miles per hour, also known as the speed of light. Today, after removing the outfit we chose and going for a run, showering, settling back into PJs, taking a nap, reading a novel, and patiently waiting for an acceptable time to head to the country club, time is moving slower than Jonny's old tortoise, Shelley.

I almost can't believe I read one of Jonny's emails out loud to Lee, even if it was just two sentences. His emails have been so many things to me over the years: comfort, entertainment, friendship, home. I've reread our emails with such frequency, I know the first few by heart.

Hey Sandy. Camp is so awesome. There is one of those big blob things we've seen in movies, where you jump and then someone jumps and shoots you up into the air into the lake. So cool!!!! Some parts are not so great, we have to chop our own wood and clean toilets and there is no AC and it's SO HOT. Also so many bugs, you would probably want to start indexing them all in search of a new species. Nerd. Just kidding!!

I looked for tortoise beetles but haven't found any yet. What am I missing back home? Please write back so I get an email every day. Ben didn't get an email and we all felt bad for him.

Jonny

Jonny,

A real life lake blob thing, I am jealous. Though I am not jealous of the toilet cleaning. I am very curious about all the bugs, even if that makes me a nerd. Without nerds there would be no email. So there.

As I've told you before, it is unlikely to find Deloyala Guttata outside of a vegetable garden or a flower bed full of Convolvulaceae. (Common Name: Morning Glories. Remember they have the flowers that look like the bell of a trumpet!)

Nothing interesting is happening at home. I finished The Great Gatsby, which I think is actually on your school reading list for this year. The novel was better than the movie, of course. Oh, someone wrote the F word on the wall in the neighborhood pool bathrooms again. I suspect it was Brock. It is super boring here, but at least I have air conditioning. Is the food any good? Camp food always looks bad in movies.

Sandy

Yeah, it's pretty bad. LOL I bet it was Brock too!! What book is up next? Will you write all my book reports for me? You're my very favorite nerd. So there. No garden or trumpet flowers at camp. But! Today I started a fire from scratch with no lighter or matches. I'm ready to go on Survivor now!

I wonder how many times in our lives he's told me I'm his favorite nerd, dork, dweeb, genius. I never minded his teasing, because it felt like an immature version of Words of Affirmation, which I read is one of five "love languages." It was an interesting book, though not very scientific. I believe that Jonny gives and receives affection using words. Words and time together. We spent so much time together throughout the ten years before I left.

I sigh and think of the latest email, which of course takes me to his photo in my album, which forces my thumb across my screen, flipping through all of his recent selfies. It's unfair and statistically impressive just how handsome he is.

His features are completely symmetrical. His hair has darkened from blond to light brown as he's aged. He keeps it short and styled, combed sort of up and to the side. He has obviously had plenty of classically masculine influences. He has a firm jaw and a strong nose, but it's really his eyes that kill us all. *Us all* being the entirety of the earth's population that is attracted to men. Because his eyes, they're wide and piercing and not fully green, but also not fully blue.

When he wears an aqua shirt?

Forget it.

Case closed. Or, as Jon Senior would joke, *Stick a fork in me, I'm done.*

It's been years since I've seen Jonny shirtless, but unfortunately, due to his past vacation photos on Instagram, I know he has kept his muscles defined. He stopped playing football after high school, despite my protests. He had the numbers to compete at the collegiate level. But Jonny didn't want to push himself so hard at an unlikely chance at the National Football League, especially when the family business was already waiting for him. Those were some of our most heated emails. I maintain my position on the matter.

Still, Jonny looks like an athlete. He bulks and bulges and could easily pick me up and carry me, as if my thin five-foot-seven frame—now with breasts!--weighs nothing.

Oh.

Now my face is flushing.

Such an odd response, blood pooling in one's cheeks for absolutely no reason.

I will never forget the first time I blushed because of him.

It was the same summer we started emailing. He'd been gone for a month, which in lonely twelve-year-old girl time is an entire eon. And he changed significantly in those billion years. I knew he was home, so I went to find him at the pool, as was our custom.

There he was, in neon board shorts, eyes shining brighter than the turquoise pool at his feet, looking tanner and—I couldn't put a word on it at the time—manlier. A month of wood chopping and fire starting made Jonny sprout muscles. It wasn't just that his appearance had changed; he was acting differently, too.

One of our songs was playing, a favorite out of the oldies playlists that the neighborhood kept on repeat. It was a Beach Boys track we always sang along to. Yet there he stood, not singing. He was talking and laughing with a girl in a bikini.

I didn't recognize her, but I hated her at first sight. It was completely irrational. I also suddenly hated my simple navy one-piece swimsuit. And I was disappointed with myself for hating a stranger and caring that he just touched her arm. Why would I care if Jonny touched some girl's arm?

I found no reasonable answer to the question.

Also I hated her because she had distinct breasts. I'd never thought about this aspect of female anatomy before, but there they were. They weren't big or bouncy or particularly noteworthy beyond their existence. Those small mounds under her pink triangle top made me furious. And the whole scene made me blush so hard my capillaries felt as if they'd burst. So did my tear ducts.

It was all very odd.

I left the pool before Jonny could spot me. I may or may not have spent an hour googling how to build up the pectoralis major muscle. You can buy a small squeeze workout tool just for this purpose, I learned. I didn't have access to my mother's Amazon account on my iPad or I would've bought myself one.

Later that night, he spotted me at the pond.

"Brainiac!" He bound up to me like he had many times before.

"Hey." I stood involuntarily and smiled a wide smile to match his, despite my tumultuous feelings.

"D'you miss me?"

"N-n-nah," I said, blushing again.

"You did." He laughed.

"So, what's the b-big news?" I asked him.

"Huh?"

"You wrote in your last email that you had big news you were going to t-t-tell me when you got home."

For the first time ever, Jonny was the one who got twitchy. "Oh, uh, it was nothing."

"D-don't be weird, Jonny. Just tell me."

"Weird?"

"Yeah. You're b-b-being strange and sweaty. More so than usual. And you keep sh-shifting your weight."

"Okay." He sat on the rickety bench, and I joined him. "Well, I finally had my first kiss, just like in that Netflix movie we watched. A girl at camp."

I felt my eyes stretch so big I must've looked like a cartoon. I adjusted my glasses. "Wow, that is b-b-b-big news." He smiled, and his chest puffed out like he was the king of the world. And he was, of my world anyway. My world, which was now being flipped on its axis. *Jonny kisses girls? Why hasn't Jonny kissed me?* I cleared my throat and managed to squeak out, "What was it like?"

"Good. A little weird, like we figured. But good. Really good."

Scientific curiosity moved my thoughts from my own emotions. "How was it weird, exactly?"

This was how we often talked about life. He would ramble about things, and I would pipe in to ask him for details, data points, specifics.

"Hmm, like, kinda sticky I guess?" I made a face. "Well, I licked my lips before. And she had on cherry Chapstick, so that kinda made it sticky. But not bad sticky, just different."

"Did your lips get stuck together?"

He laughed. "No, her Chapstick just rubbed off on me."

"Does cherry Chapstick taste good?"

"Yeah, I think so."

"Huh. That does ssssound weird."

After a beat, he said, "Yeah, but...well, you'll understand in a few years."

"O-k-kay." I wanted to understand right that second. But then Brock and Nash and two other boys arrived on their bikes. Off we went to play *Legend of Zelda*, as if my thoughts weren't scattering in one million sad, confused directions.

That wasn't the moment I fell for Jonny, of course, since I was only twelve. But it was the start of a snowball that would pick up size and speed until it rolled right over my soul. Repeatedly.

That's why tonight is so important.

Tonight is it.

I can't carry on anymore, living with my heart pumping outside of my chest, in the hands of a boy who might never hand me his in return. Worse still, I think he knows he has all my dreams and emotions and confusion tucked in his back pocket. Or he did in the past. He had to at least suspect it.

Reflexively, I pull up the first Knife Email, as I call them. The first in a series of messages that produce a distinct stabbing sensation in my stomach. I imagined I was bleeding out at my small purple desk tucked under my Pottery Barn Teen loft bed. I know it's neither helpful nor productive to re-read them, but what does productivity have to do with heartache?

> *Sandy,*
> *Remember that girl I told you about, Layla? The one who was at camp and goes to school with me now—Brock was staring at her in Algebra like he wanted to kiss her, and that pissed me off. She and I have only kissed the one time, but I think I want to ask her to be my girlfriend. Is that stupid?*

He asked me that question a lot throughout our lives. What I gathered he was really asking, over and over, was, "Am I as stupid as my brother says I am?" And I always answered with a resounding, "No." When it came to Layla, however, I wanted to scream, *Yes! Yes, it's stupid! She will never love you as much as I do, even if she's a sophomore with breasts who doesn't stutter, who gets to see you every day in your Algebra class!*

Instead, I looked at the data available to me and told him my conclusion.

> *Jonny,*
> *When you and Brock are staring at Layla, who is Layla staring at? Was the previous kiss that memorable? If you want to kiss her again, and don't want her to be able to kiss anyone else, I suppose making her your girlfriend would be the smart move.*
> *Sandy*

I'd cried when I hit send that day. I didn't want him to ask Layla to be his girlfriend, but I didn't want him to feel dumb. Most importantly, I didn't want him to stop writing to me. At that point in our friendship, I thought maybe he just didn't know how I felt about him. I was his "little sister," after all, only thirteen. I was so thin I resembled the hanging skeleton in my biology class, if one added frizzy bangs to the head and braces to the teeth. Conversely, Jonny *could drive his own car!* I was in the troposphere while he was rocketing through the exosphere. Totally different stratospheric levels.

But the next year, I got the feeling he knew. I arrived in the halls of the high school, eyes wide and constantly searching the large, linoleum-floored spaces for him. To my delight, we even shared a class. At just fourteen, I was already taking junior English, and so was Jonny, an actual junior.

His face lit up when he saw me in class on the first day, but he didn't make a move to sit by me. He enjoyed having me there for educational purposes, since I'd already read all the assigned books, most of them more than once. Neither of us would ever actually cheat, but I was generous with my insights and suggestions.

Early on that year, in that class, some of the junior girls were getting bold with their disgust for me. Since I clearly had the upper hand where brainpower was concerned, they zeroed in on all of the other aspects they could.

Why don't you straighten your hair, sweetie?

That must be your brother's big, smelly sweatshirt, right? So adorable.

Even though you're smart, it must be so awkward for you to read these really grown-up concepts.

Loving those boots, I had them three years ago when I was little, too.

That was the day I actually fell in full-fledged romantic love with Jonny Canton, because he, in all his teal-eyed, firm-bodied, football-jersey-wearing magnificence, shifted to form a wall between those girls and me. With an uncharacteristic seriousness I'll never forget, he told them off—loudly.

"We get it. You're all jealous of her. She's smarter than you'll ever be, and you're insecure. Knock it off, unless you want me telling the whole school how you're intimidated by a freshman." He grunted at them in anger and turned to me. "You good, Sandy?"

I nodded and looked away quickly as he took the seat next to mine. For a few weeks, he sat by me in class, until the teenage hormonal storm had blown over. Then he returned to his spot with the other jocks in the back of the room.

During the first semester of that year, I suspect looking back now, Jonny caught on that I looked at him the way he looked at Layla. Thus, Knife Email number two arrived on an unsuspecting Friday night.

Earlier in the week, I had sent him a few articles about our current reading assignment with a totally casual, scientifically curious question about him and Layla. I'd seen them holding hands in the hall again. I had only tripped a little bit, both physically and metaphorically. Holding hands didn't mean anything, or at least it didn't mean *everything,* did it?

Last we'd discussed her, months ago, she was flirting with every guy on the team except for him, so he'd asked me if he should break things off. I reasoned he absolutely should. But after witnessing the hand-holding, his reply made me feel like he was trying to gently hand my heart back to me, realizing he was holding it and completely uncomfortable with its weight of about ten ounces.

> *Sandy,*
>
> *Thanks for your help on the Fahrenheit 451 paper. I got a B minus! Yeah, Layla and I are back together. She said she was sorry. You understand, right? Cuz aren't you hot for that guy in the orchestra with you? It's time you got that first kiss, Sand. I think you've maybe been waiting around for someone special and you shouldn't do that anymore. You're in high school now! Date guys! Kiss guys! Have fun!*
>
> *See you at the brunch after church on Sunday with our parents. Let's hope they have our favorite mini quiches again. And that my old Aunt Martha doesn't come. I can't eat when our table is surrounded by her terrible perfume cloud. She smells like dead flowers and cleaning supplies! Barf!*
>
> *Jonny*

I threw my iPad across the room that day and promised myself I'd never let Jonny affect me so much again. I knew I was ill-equipped for that promise. I'd let him break my heart again. More than once.

But all that ends tonight. Hopefully.

CHAPTER 3

"You look nice," my mother says lightly as I enter the kitchen. T-minus one hour until I can head to the club. My parents are packing up to leave already.

"Thanks," I say with a smile.

My mother cocks her head at me in that scientific way that we share. She is smarter, prettier, and just as quietly introverted as me, but somehow less awkward. I admire her and love her fiercely, but that doesn't mean I've never wished she was more like other moms.

While she has spent my life literally curing cancer, or attempting to do so with her research, I have been desperate for someone to tell me what to wear, how to do something called contour with makeup, and how to make my hair wavy instead of frizzy. I have always longed to be a girly girl, but my mother didn't have any insights. She focused on her goals and encouraged me to do the same. Anytime I would get depressed or complain about my wardrobe, she would redirect my thoughts to the blessing that is my intellect and, of course, the responsibility of such a blessing.

Not to say she wasn't also loving. In their way, my parents gushed over me. They had no qualms about speech therapy and traditional therapy to help me accept and calm my stutter. They spared no expense for extra books, the latest apps, special tests, and any scientific gadget I asked for. And my mother tried to be there for me emotionally, as best she could. So I'm not surprised when she clears her throat and forces our eye contact.

"Do you know he's going to be there?" she asks.

"What?" I try to say with an airy, casual laugh.

"I mean have you heard from him? Jonny?"

I look anywhere but at her light hazel eyes that match my own. "Yes, he asked if I was coming."

"Oh, okay."

I look up at her, unsure about her tone. My parents have never expressed anything but distant approval when it comes to Jonny and our friendship. I decide not to ask and move instead to grab a bottled water from the fridge.

"Just know that your father and I are so excited you're back. OU's School of Medicine is excellent."

"I know, Mom," I say, turning back to see what her face might be saying that her words aren't. She clears her throat again.

"Good. Who knows where your residency will take you? So we really want you close by for a while." She squeezes my hand, but she might as well be squeezing my lungs, because I am struggling to breathe.

Without saying so, she's just called glaring attention to what none of us have ever said aloud. The truth of the matter is Jonny is the reason I agreed to graduate early. He's the real reason I moved 1,600 miles away for college, even though Stanford wasn't my first choice. He's the real reason I didn't come home over multiple breaks and holidays.

40

He's the reason for a million minuscule things. For example, how I got my first French kiss. It was a Knife Email.

I still had only kissed three guys throughout high school. It had been severely underwhelming. I had been assuring myself that someday Jonny would come to his senses and see how perfect we were for each other and *his* lips wouldn't be chapped and scratchy. *He* wouldn't smell like burrito fumes covered under too many sprays of Cool Water cologne. *He* wouldn't smash onto me and then walk away in some sort of confused, hormonal, drive-by pecking.

But one night my brother was home when my parents were out. And there were noises coming from his room. Not sure what I was hearing, I emailed my person about it.

> *JONNY!*
> *I think Eric is humping a girl in his room right now! I hear thumping and moaning and some kind of slapping noise? Are they slapping each other? And sloppy wet sounds? This is unsettling! I am going to vomit.*
> *Why are so many movies and books and even songs about intercourse, when sex is clearly the most confusing, disgusting, disturbing thing in the whole galaxy?!*

Jon's reply was quick.

> *LOL, Sand, trust me, it's not.*

Three little words, contracted.
It is not.

My senses dulled that night. Colors paled, sounds quieted.

Jonny had been with someone, with Layla probably. *Been with!* As in coitus! Intercourse! S-E-X! Love-making!

No, surely not that last one. That was for adults.

The next day, puffy-eyed and distraught, I let Alan Vu kiss me with his tongue in one of the orchestra's practice rooms. He had apologized for his previous drive-by approach and had been asking me to go out with him for a long time, so I conceded. He was careful and slow, and I let him put his hand under my shirt. Not that there was anything for him to find there, but even so, I think it was the best day of his life.

Until I burst into tears and ran out of the room.

That night I informed my parents I was done with high school.

And I was. I'd been done with high school coursework for a year. I was well into my college classes. I found a spring internship program for incoming freshmen, applied for late admission, and left. My mother asked if I was going to say goodbye to Jonny at Sunday lunch, since he was driving up from OU's Norman campus, but I didn't. I couldn't. We never discussed the details.

I just had to get away.

Four states away. As soon as possible.

A lot of good it did me.

The increase in miles seemed to correlate directly with the increase of words, flowing electronically between Jonny and me, for the next two years. When I removed myself from his life, he missed me. He didn't hold back about his feelings. He never did.

Sand,

I'm not at all surprised you got into a special internship and your fancy-pants school, but I can't believe you

*didn't say bye. Sunday lunch sucks without you. How am
I going to survive three years of them?*
Jonny

In an exercise of mental toughness, which I had been studying at that time, I mustered all of my willpower, clung to any and all distractions, and waited a whole week before replying. I decided from then on to take more of a clinical approach. I would only email him weekly, as scheduled. I would step back emotionally and simply read about his life, ask questions, and share anything of interest.

As if my decision could save me from the digital pixels' effects.

*J - Undergraduate degrees at United States universities
are four-year programs. I'm concerned you don't know
this when you are a sophomore in one such program
yourself. - S*

---

*Well, I'm a dum-dum business major at OU, not a pre-
med genius at Stanford, what'd you expect?! I expect
there's no way you don't graduate early, Brainiac. Three
years, max. When is your first trip home?*

---

*Please do not call my best friend a dum-dum. So you've
decided on business? Are you certain that is what YOU
want and not what Jon Senior wants? Like I have said a
thousand times, Canton Cards can survive without you,
if you can't survive with it.*

And I am not certain when I'm headed home. I need to get settled here.

Jonny wasn't deep or pensive by nature, especially not with anyone who wasn't me. I suppose he could have gotten deep with Layla or his rebound girls through the years, but I doubted it. Everyone liked Good Time Jonny, Cut Up Jonny, Football Star Jonny. I imagined, in my weakest moments, that girls liked Great Sex Jonny.

I just liked Jonny. During my freshman year at Stanford, he morphed from Jonny to Jon before my eyes as I read each syllable he sent.

Sand,

I've been thinking about it a lot. I don't think it's the business I dislike, I think it's my role. Rob the Robot talks spreadsheets and projections all day long, but really, I think the whole business is about people. Is that stupid? I mean think about it, why do gift cards exist? To send a note to someone. And who buys our cards? Not like at the store I mean the big orders—shop owners like Blaine's dad. When I talk to him about his shops, he lights up like you when you talk about bugs. OKAY, I know you're over bugs now... Like you when you talk about how many bones are in one foot alone.

And who runs our storefronts in every city? Regular people like me or like dad.

Not like Rob.

My brother is just not good with people, and I'm worried it's starting to affect things.

Dad seems stressed.

Sure, Rob's smarter than me, but does that mean he should automatically take over for Dad?

What if he's not a good fit?

What if I am?

- J

J-

Not stupid.

Rob may have a high IQ, but his EQ is zero. Less than zero. Your EQ is off the charts, though you know I dislike that term's lack of specificity. I think your brother always chastises you because he knows it's the truth. You've got a gift for interacting with people, Jonny. Everyone is drawn to you like insects to blue light. They can't help it. You see people, read them, and know how to talk to them, to put them at ease.

This seems like a very desirable quality for a leader and a salesman.

Seems like a vital quality in a CEO.

- S

CEO?! Now you're just talking crazy talk. When are you coming home?

Aunt Martha misses you so much.

- J

We wrote a lot about who we wanted to be and what we wanted to do. We wrote about our favorite summer memories. We shared funny things that happened in class or on campus. He talked about frat parties sometimes. I shared about Lee and Avery and our late nights in the library.

We never wrote about dating. I suspected he was dating constantly, and I guessed he knew that I was not dating at all. I enjoyed my studies too much. And the guys around me seemed to be just as focused as me.

Last year, the final Knife Email arrived.

> *Sandy,*
> *I talked to Carly about everything with Rob and how he blew up at me last month. She agrees with you. If my best friend and my girlfriend agree, it's legit, right? So I'm going to talk to Dad about all of it. Are you coming home for Thanksgiving? Carly wants to meet you!*
> *Jon*

That afternoon I took an emotional journey through the stages of grief via Jonny's Instagram profile and Lee's beer mini fridge. There she was, tagging him in all her photos. Jonny had been with a new girl every month for forever, but there it was, a pattern with Carly.

She was a classically beautiful redhead with aqua eyes. Which was just incomprehensible. That was Jonny's striking characteristic. Two people with eyes like that shouldn't get together and disrupt the entirety of human iris genetics.

Later that evening, Lee dragged me to a party, and in a sad, drunken haze, I experienced penetration, technically losing my virginity. It was only a technicality, by my estimation, because Dylan, our cute friend from Physiology, had just gotten started before I felt a rush of emotion and fled. It took days to sort through the feelings. Shame, guilt, embarrassment, frustration, regret.

Regret.

As was our custom—though I'm not sure Jonny was aware—after a Knife Email, I'd close my emotions and thoughts off from Jonny for a few weeks. I would then return to him with deep questions birthed from my time of reflection.

Jonny,
Do you still believe humans have souls?

Sand,
Of course. We gave ours to Jesus when we were in middle school, remember? #MightytoSave
Have you changed your beliefs? Again, why do you bother asking me such deep questions—aren't you surrounded by geniuses? - J

J -
As previously explained in detail, I value your opinion, on any and all subjects. That won't change no matter whom I am surrounded by.

I maintain that position. I've read extensively and de-cided I do still believe in souls. There is something un-quantifiable about our mortal existence. I believe the human body is indeed too "wonderfully made" to not have been by intelligent design. The memory of Pastor Tim—#HowGreatIsOurGod—leads me to my next ques-tion: do you believe what he warned us of during his an-nual purity sermon series—do you think two souls join together when people have sex?

S

Shit. Warn a guy. Hmmm... Does it make me sound like a pussy if I say yes? I guess. But I kinda think they do, yes.

Jonny,

As agreed upon five years ago, every time you use the word pussy to imply weakness, I need to remind you how powerful the vagina is. It is highly elastic, can double its size, and revert back to its original state. It is self-cleaning. It can push out a ten-, eleven-, or even thirteen-pound baby. (There are larger babies on re-cord, but it is unclear if they were delivered via C-sec-tion.)

The world's strongest vagina, possessed by a Russian gymnast and mother, can lift nearly thirty-one pounds. I'm resisting the urge to attach photos.

- S

SANDY, WARN A GUY!!!!

I don't believe I'm a prude, nor am I a religious zealot, but I do believe sex is beyond a physical act. There has to be something spiritual about it. I believe it could be argued that intercourse is a union of two souls. If that's not the case, why does sex feel so singularly intimate? Why did it make me feel so vulnerable?

And I wasted my first union in a smoky, dimly lit backroom in the basement of some pre-med girl's cousin's house with a guy who tasted like fish and reeked of marijuana.

That is not what I had envisioned for my first time.

I'd always planned on waiting for marriage. Because of course I was going to marry Jonny. We'd meet at the altar at our neighborhood church where we'd knelt on Wednesday nights during our religious phase as tweens. We would have our childhood pastor, who baptized each of us, do the ceremony. Then that night Jonny would show me just how *not* confusing and disgusting sex is. It was going to be perfect.

In my extreme state, I'd completely abandoned the dream.

Lee said I was liberated from my anglo-patriarchal religious suppression. (She's from the East Coast.) Avery said I'd just gotten "a dud" out of the way so I could move on to the good stuff.

But I didn't move on.

I never did, and I'm scared I never will.

After Carly, Jonny was Jon, and paragraphs turned into sentences, then words, then memes and selfies. Still, he always replied.

And he followed up on his own when I went silent, checking on me.

My emotions reached extreme levels with every red, bold **(1)** that appeared on top of my Mac's mail icon. They still do, no matter how much I try to reason with myself. I only use that email account for Jonny, and it is the only app or account to ever produce an audible notification on my phone or iPad or computer.

Carly eventually made her departure from Jonny's Instagram, and other girls rotated through in her place, but none for quite as long. Then Jonny deactivated his account as he got more established within the family business. After all, he had dreams of expanding Canton Cards internationally. He no longer has time for filters and dance videos.

So as far as I know, Jonny is single.

And he wrote that wanted me to come tonight.

He wants to see me.

This is it. I will tell him, clearly and calmly, how I feel. Given our history and compatibility, it is logical for us to at least try going on a date. We owe that to ourselves. He'll either agree or disagree.

If he agrees, tonight becomes the best night of my life.

If he disagrees, I officially shut down my feelings for him.

And, in the event of the latter, as I just assured to my mother with a slow nod, I will not to flee the state again.

No matter how badly I may want to.

CHAPTER 4

Deep breaths.

Practiced words.

A scientific approach.

I grip the steering wheel excessively as I practice. "Jonny, I want to talk to you. I have an interesting idea. Exsssperiment, even."

Deep breath, c'mon!

"Jonny, I have an interesting idea for an experiment, for us. We are best friends. The best of the best. But looking at our long history, and our obvious compatibility, I think we should at least attempt to date...romantically. D-d-d— shit!" I tap the air conditioning button until it blows the air at maximum speed. "I think we should at least attempt to date romantically. Don't you? Don't you? Don't you?"

I repeat the hard sections a few more times.

I'm pleased. The suggestion is simple and leaves no room for misinterpretation. It is also short and memorized.

I park my car and steal one last glance in my mirror. Avery insisted I try a new mascara that would make my eyes "pop." While it did lengthen my lashes, it also flaked off, directly into my contacts. I couldn't get my eyes to stop watering, causing more of the offensive flaking. So tonight I'm forced to wear my glasses. Unfortunate, since Jonny has never seen me in my contacts, but not insurmountable.

At least these are cute new frames.

And again, breasts. I have those now.

I walk into the country club—a big, red-bricked mansion with white columns and colorful, lush landscaping—somewhat prepared for the cacophony that greets me. The club's go-to oldies music station. Hundreds of voices filling room after room. The smell of flowers. And barbecue. Too many colognes and perfumes.

It's not surprising that I slip in and around totally unnoticed. I don't mind anymore. There was a time in middle school when I would race home and try to talk to one of my brothers, just to confirm that I wasn't actually invisible. In high school, I'd stomp into the middle of our backyard and scream as loudly as possible at the sky to make sure my vocal cords still worked.

Those were hormonal times.

Hormones toy with one's emotions, and emotions cause even the most logical among us to behave irrationally.

In college, I realized I didn't mind standing on the outside of a situation looking in. Large crowds can be wonderful for an introvert. I can observe and ponder without having to actually talk about myself or talk in general. Lee and Avery forced me to talk anyway and now like to take most of the credit for the disappearance of my stutter.

"Forget your fancy speech therapy. You need roomie shock therapy," Lee would say before dragging me into a conversation with an older classmate or a cute boy.

Here, tonight, I'm actually happy to blend in with the recently renovated walls. So many around me are acquaintances I don't care to talk to. And though curiosity may prompt them to ask about me and Stanford and medical school, what they're really asking is—as if I am an alien species they've been able to make first contact with—*what's it like to have such a big, fast brain? To be so different?* I don't know, Mrs. Jones, what's it like to be so dull?

Best to just stay in the background until I find Jonny.

But he's not here.

I make lap after lap through the outdoor festivities and all of the open rooms inside. I check my email again and again. I eat a little meat chunk wrapped in a second type of meat. Bacon, I think? I regret it. I chat politely with my parents and a few of their friends, begrudgingly.

I spot Jon Senior and his wife a few times, as well as Rob. Cantons are always surrounded by crowds waiting for a few moments of their time. But none of the cells of chatter feature Jonny as their nucleus. Surely, he's coming. This is his own family's ridiculous party!

It's almost dark when I'm circling quickly through the giant covered porch again, ignoring the sweeping view of the golf course under the setting sun. I'm sweating and tense. I hear a deep voice call my name somewhere to my right. I look with my head but keep moving forward, missing the brain-body connection others seem to have mastered.

I am suddenly freezing.

And wet.

Because I've collided with a server carrying a huge pitcher of a thick, dark red liquid. Whatever it is, it's no longer in the pitcher. The goo is all over my hair and shirt. Thankfully the server didn't drop the pitcher. I apologize to her as she apologizes to me. At least no glass broke, and no loud commotion was made.

No one noticed.

Except the source of that voice.

"Squirt?"

My brother.

I shudder, more from frustration than the chill.

"Hey! Squirt!" Deon smiles down at me. He's a year older than Jonny, and his thin, tall frame matches my own, though it's filled out considerably since I saw him last. He looks handsome. Happy. We've never been particularly close, but it is nice to see him. He draws near enough to see the aftermath around my feet. "Oh, shit, Sand, what happened?"

"Raspberry concentrate?" I ask the server. She nods apologetically before turning back the way she came.

"Here." Before I can protest, Deon has whipped off his tee shirt for me, leaving him in the white tank he wears under his shirts. "I can go grab a polo from one of the golf guys in a minute."

I sigh. It's a very sweet gesture. "Thanks, D."

"Of course." I quickly put his vintage red shirt on over my entire torso and slip out of my soiled top. The extremely soft fabric of Deon's shirt has an old-school patriotic print. It's clean and doesn't reek of artificially flavored sugar sludge. But it dwarfs me.

"Welcome home, Squirt. How you been?" I decide I should just find a tank top from the same golf shop he mentioned. Surely they will have something cuter than this. I turn to ask my brother to lead the way.

"Sandy!"

Now that's the deep voice I was waiting for.

This is it.

I turn to face my best friend, my smile already invading my cheeks.

But before I can spot him I see...Layla?

"Sorry we're so late!" he calls from behind her, following with, I now see, their fingers linked together.

"Yeah, sorry, Sandra. That's, uh, my bad," Layla says to me and to my brother, with a tone that implies she may or may not have been having sex with Jonny moments ago. I shudder anew.

"Sand, it's so good to—" Jonny lets go of Layla's manicured hand and reaches to hug me but shrinks away when notices my dripping hair. "What...what's that?"

I am frozen. Figuratively. Unable to...anything.

"Raspberry concentrate," Deon answers for me.

"Ohhh, that's what I smell!" Layla giggles freely. "Hey, Deon, good to see you."

For a moment I can envision my hopeless plight through the eyes of my brother. I'm staring with longing at Jonny, who is staring lovingly at Layla, who is looking at my brother flirtatiously from under her long, curled lashes.

I suspect she uses mascara that doesn't flake.

"You too, Layla. Jon. Been a while, man." My brother reaches out to shake Jon's hand as if they're both khaki-clad forty-five-year-olds. Jonny will look amazing when he's forty-five.

"Yeah, D, forever. How are you?"

"Good, good, you know, just glad I managed to graduate last year, before Einstein here. Will would've never let me hear the end of that." Deon is correct. My oldest brother would have teased him endlessly. I wish he hadn't said it, though, because now...

"Wait, you graduated?" Layla's top lip curls up in a way I like because it makes her look unintelligent. I am not in a good mental or emotional state. Have I even said hello?

I am able to nod and almost smile.

"The brainiac in the flesh. Graduated in three years, as predicted. It's so good to see you!" Jonny looks at me with his signature magnetism. It's enough for me to block out his hand-holding with the enemy.

"You, too," I say with a genuine smile and no double with the *T. Victory!*

"Wow, and you left high school early as it is, right? I mean, that's amazing, Sandra. Congratulations!" Layla seems genuine, which irks me further. "Oh, c'mon, Jon, your dad's waving us over."

"Is he? You're right. Damn, I love this girl." Jon smiles at her in an altogether different way than he smiles at me. "What would I do without her?" I feel my brother's eyes ping-ponging between us. "I'll catch you later, Sand, okay?" Jonny's promise is a half-hearted holler over his shoulder as Layla drags him away.

No. You will not catch me later. Because I cannot stay here another minute.

I make my way out to my car, accosted by the boom of nearby fireworks.

"I love this girl."

Boom.

That girl.

Boom.

Not me.

Boom. Boom.

Never me.

Boom. Boom. Boom.

It wasn't sent electronically, but the words were a knife all the same.

The last knife.

This is the last heartbreak.

"I mean it this time!" I sob to myself as I slump into my steering wheel.

Myself believes me.

Almost.

CHAPTER 5

Lee: So, is spring semester going any better than fall semester?

Avery: Yeah, you've been back from Christmas break for weeks and nada!

Lee: She was recovering from avoiding certain someones at home all break.

Avery: LEE!!! We are not discussing that!

Me: What Avery said.

Me: I've just been adjusting. This semester will be even harder, I think, but still it's interesting, stimulating, intimidating...

Me: I love it.

Lee: Any hot guys in these classes?

Avery: YAS, Lee, now that's the line of questioning we need!

Me: I haven't had a chance to notice yet.

Avery: That's BS!

Lee: Get your head out of your books and look around.

Avery: Yeah, you need a rebound.

Me: I don't have time for a rebound.

Lee: A study buddy then. Just don't go Full Hermit for another full semester, smartypants.

Me: Understood.

Avery: We love you, Doc.

Me: Love you back, Docs.

I tuck my phone into my back pocket as I enter the freezing lecture hall for Anatomy II. My friends' words fresh in my mind, I take the time to actually look around. Everyone around me looks exhausted and not completely unafraid. I wonder if I look the same. It is probable.

I start to slouch into a seat and realize everyone's shuffling to the front to pick up our first tests. I make my way to the desk where the TA is handing back the slips of paper. I stare at the back of the shoes ahead of me in line and let my mind wander to the two questions on the test that I was unsure about.

"Name?" I don't hear him. "Um, first, last, either will do?"

I look up.

Wow.

My breath catches.

The deep brown eyes that meet mine are intense and beautiful, matching the grace and symmetry of the face they rest in.

"Hayes," I say clearly, without stumbling, surprising myself.

"You're Sandra," he smiles wide.

Wow, again! Double wow!

I nod.

"Best score in the class."

I feel all my body's blood rush to the tiny veins laying atop my cheekbones for no scientific purpose.

"Best in all the Anatomy II classes, actually." He stands and looks down at me. He reaches his large hand out to clasp mine. His long fingers are dexterous. I wonder if they're future-surgeon hands. "I'm Wade. Anderson. Fourth Year. Nice to meet you."

"Sandra." I smile, feeling my cheeks burn brighter as he releases me.

"I know." He smirks with confidence. I think I laugh as I turn and journey back to my seat.

I feel a tingling sensation in my chest. A sensation I've only felt once before in all my twenty years. The feeling terrifies and excites me. Maybe there is hope for me after all. Not for love or a future or anything crazy. But maybe I can, in fact, have a rebound.

I watch Wade as the other students retrieve their tests. I can tell other girls noticed his appeal weeks ago. Some flirt. One girl is wearing a sweater dress so short she will surely die of hypothermia during the duration of this class. All the lecture halls are like iceboxes. This is a fact.

I watch her as she approaches him. She bats long eyelashes and smiles wide. She's completely comfortable in her tanned skin. She has long blond hair and dark eyes. Something about the way she carries herself reminds me of Layla.

I notice Wade noticing Not Layla and said questionable dress. He is generous with his smiles and encouragement. I don't like the exchange.

But I do like that he doesn't stand up for anyone else.

Me: Okay, I took your advice yesterday and looked up.

Lee: AND?

Avery: AND????

Me: Hot TA. Like a less broody Ian Somerhalder.

Lee: The vampire?

Avery: He's an actor, Lee. Vampires aren't real. LOL

Me: I said less broody! Less cold. Like a happy, warm Ian.

Me: Fourth year. I think he might be perfect.

Lee: Oh boy. Wasn't Teal-Eyed Chris Pratt "perfect"?

Avery: YOU DARE SPEAK HIS NAME.

Lee: I didn't say his name!

Me: I don't even know who you're referencing?

Avery: I don't care if this guy is a werewolf dragon king. I'm just glad you're back on the dating horse!

Avery: Climb back in that saddle!

Lee: Giddy up, cowgirl.

Avery: Ride him! lololol

Me: This escalated quickly.

Avery: LOLOL yeehaw, bitchesssss.

Me: Oh my. First, let's discuss: how can I NOT blend in with the wall this time? Because I met him before class and I thought he might be flirting, but then he didn't look at me once during his lecture.

Avery: Better clothes.

Lee: Better hair, makeup.

Avery: Be more outgoing, smiley.

Lee: Don't show off in class.

Me: Wow, please, don't feel that you need to hold back on account of my feelings.

Lee: [wince emoji]

Avery: Sorry! Just be yourself and talk to him. Actually initiating conversation would be a great first step.

Lee: Agreed. But pluck your eyebrows.

Avery: OMG yes, definitely pluck your eyebrows.

Me: I dislike you both.

For two weeks I have been nervous, calmed red cheeks, made eye contact, and worn my tightest thick jeans. Tight, lined pants are the best I can do in these temperatures. Even my cute sweaters or tight, long-sleeve tees are usually buried under a giant hoodie. That girl with the dresses is obviously mentally unstable. Surely Wade notices her sheer desperation.

But he doesn't seem to notice me.

Or he's just as tired and anxious as every other med school student I've met. Probably more so since he is a TA on top of his fourth-year studies.

I've corresponded with Lee and Avery about my situation, but they are not much help. Their suggestions are good in theory, but in actuality, neither of them is much more trendy or flirty than myself. We know how to be great friends via group text, get stellar grades, play a stringed instrument, and find humorous medicine-related memes. Avery claims to be very knowledgeable about sex but not dating. That's the extent of our combined skill set.

The chime of my mail app snaps me back to the text I'm supposed to be studying. My eyes dart around with a ready apology, but no one is near me in the library. I find my phone underneath a notebook that's underneath an open textbook.

Reflexively, I scroll through our last few messages, spread over five months.

Jonny,
Layla, again?
-Sandy

Sandy,
Really? We haven't seen each other in over a year, and
you bail after the fireworks?? And yes. She's changed.
Jon

I waited weeks to reply in protest to the notion that Layla would ever change enough to be worthy of him.

J-
This 2018 University of Denver study found that some-
one is three times more likely to cheat if they have cheat-
ed in the past. [link]
- S

In anger, I assume, he waited weeks to reply me.

Sand, we were just kids. People grow up. Someday you'll
meet someone and you'll understand. - Jon

I found it noteworthy that he didn't ask, "Is that stupid?" about reuniting with her, as he normally would. I surmised this was either because he no longer valued my opinion or he didn't want to hear my opinion, knowing what it would be.

"Someday you'll understand."

That sentence put the nail in my Hopes and Dreams with Jonny Coffin. *Someday* because even though we are both college graduates, he'll never see me as an equal, a counterpart. I will forever be categorized as the geeky little neighbor who knows nothing about tornadoes and everything about grasshopper exoskeletons.

I didn't respond to him at all after that. He sent a selfie or two, which I ignored. My parents begged me to go with them to the annual Canton Christmas party and the club's New Year's Eve party, but I managed to refrain. I went the entire holiday break without running into him or Layla. It was a triumph, even though I felt anything but triumphant.

> *Sandy,*
> *Merry Christmas! I missed you at the party, but I under-*
> *stand you're very busy with med school, even over the*
> *break. Geniuses gonna genius, right? - J*

I didn't respond. I managed to mend my heart and retrain my brain with each week that we didn't email. If he loved Layla, then he could email her.

But I missed my best friend.

I still do, desperately, as I pull up the message that's just arrived.

> *So, how's med school?*
> *Please write back.*
> *-J*

The letters on the screen make me think of his teal eyes, which makes me wonder about the deep brown eyes of late. An idea strikes me. I type and send the thought before I can examine it rationally.

> *Busy. Actually, I need your help with something. A new experiment. Can we get coffee as soon as you're available? - Sandy*

> *Well, call me a cow and tip me over, you need MY help? I'll dust off the old lab coat you got me. I can come down to the city tomorrow? - Jon*

We reply back and forth to choose the time and location. I smile as I put my phone away. If I want to be magnetic, approachable, memorable, likable, there's no better teacher in the world than Jonny Canton.

CHAPTER 6

"**B**rainiac!" His smile lights up his whole perfect face. I will my cardiovascular system to remain calm, but it does not. Will I ever be able to fully retrain my neural pathways when it comes to thoughts of him? Evidence suggests this is unlikely.

My palms grow slick with sweat as he makes his way across the cafe where, of course, I arrived first. In my haste to discuss this idea, I scheduled our coffee in between classes, with no time to go home and swap my glasses for contacts. The corner cafe is attached to a clinic and is cold and crowded. I have to keep my big sweatshirt on, and the small space is too bright and too loud. *Who cares about any of that? This is just coffee with a friend! C'mon, synapses, work with me!*

"Hi!" I beam a huge smile right back at him. This time he doesn't hesitate to pull me out of my seat to hug me, since, unlike the last time I saw him, my hair is not covered in scarlet goo. It is a long hug, my favorite kind. It gives me the opportunity to smell his classic spring fresh shampoo, his Acqua di Giò cologne, and a hint of the smell of ten-year-old boys during the summer I am probably imagining. My subconscious seems to have greatly benefited from the mental toughness exercises.

Jonny pulls back from our hug. "Man, you could've just left for Stanford yesterday. You never change a bit." I feel my face twitch. "Which I'm glad for! Why mess with perfection, right, Doc?"

I relax and nod as we sit.

He looks at our table supporting two cups. "You started drinking coffee finally?"

"Freshman year. I couldn't have survived without it."

He smirks. "Black?"

"No, I maintain that the Black Death you drink is disgusting. I drink flavored lattes, like a sane person." He laughs, and something almost fractures in my sternum. It's been almost two years since I've heard it, but it's still my favorite sound.

"Hey, I'm the insane person *you* called for help. And damn. It's been too long, Sandy. How've you been? Is this"—he motions toward the windows where the buildings of OU School of Medicine can be seen—"all you hoped it'd be?"

"So far, yes. It really is." I push my glasses back up my nose. "And you? How's your official position under Rob?"

"Well, thanks to the suggestions of someone very smart," he dips his chin at me, "I'm not actually under him."

"Jonny! That's great news!"

"Eh, I'm just a regional manager, doing the same thing I've always done, traveling to meet potential franchisees, helping shop owners, sales really. Same ol'. But at least Dad made it clear to my brother that we're equal partners, him in the office with Dad, me in the field with my uncle, *not* boss and employee." I beam at him. His older brother is, as Avery would say, a total asshat.

"Sorry I didn't make it to your graduation." I mean it, but he shrugs casually.

"You had your own, smarty pants. I knew that." We both sip our coffee. I wait, knowing he will jump to fill the silence first. "So? What's our experiment? Lab coat doesn't fit anymore."

I laugh, imagining him in the small dress-up lab coat costume I got him when he was fourteen. I take a deep breath and speak the words I planned. I clear my throat.

"I need you to t-t-teach me how to be more personable." It was a complete, direct thought. But Jonny looks confused.

"You're personable."

I shake my head. "Personable like you, approachable, fun, memorable." I can see the skepticism on his face. "There is a g-guy," I add.

"Ohhhhh!" He smiles a mischievous smile that looks just like the variety my older brothers often threw my way. It's not my favorite of his smiles, but it still causes my own grin to make an appearance. "Sandy Hayes finally has a crush. This is amazing."

"Ughhh." I cover my reddening face with my hands. "I have enlisted the wrong person."

"No! No, I'm sorry. I'm happy to help. How did you envision this crush *experiment* would work?"

I peek at him through my fingers. He has calmed himself.

"Well, I hadn't planned past this conversation. I want you to explain to me how I can be like you."

He twists his features into an overly smug scoff. "Psh, I'm not sure all this can be taught." We both laugh. "Seriously, though, I'm not sure. You know me, I just talk to people, smile...chat."

"You know I hate to chat."

"I do." He is smirking again.

"Jonny, come on, you have to have better advice than to start up small talk with him."

"What's his name?"

"Wade."

"Okay, bit of a tool name, but I guess he didn't pick it. And you met him in class?" I nod. "Well, honestly, Sand, yes, small talk."

This line of thought is futile. Jonny is a force when he enters a room; people approach him. He doesn't have to meander up to someone and start talking. I need a new approach.

"Here is a better question." *Deep inhale. Take your time.* "What made you n-notice Layla?"

Jonny's eyebrows threaten to depart the top of his face. He gives his head a quick shake. "Did not see that question coming." I appreciate that he ignored my stutter, like always, but I'm irritated at myself for getting worked up. I fist my hands under the table and wait for him to continue. "Okay, I get what you're asking. Let me think. Damn, that was a long time ago."

"Eight years. At summer camp."

Jonny nods, accustomed to the blessing and curse that is my very detailed, very accurate memory. "Right. She came up to me and oh! She asked me for help." He stares at a wall to our left, reliving the moment.

His Layla Smile arrives in our conversation. I breathe through the resulting stabbing sensation in the vicinity of my appendix.

"I remember it now." Even his voice softens. *This is fine. This is nothing new! I'm interested in Wade, not Jonny!* I lean in despite my instinct to recoil. "I felt like a million bucks because she, the pretty blond girl, was asking me, little scrawny ol' me, for help with her tent. After that I swore I could've fought a bear by hand."

"Unlikely." I don't even smirk, but as he comes back to the present, he laughs loudly.

"That's a solid first tactic to try, though, isn't it? Can you ask him for help in class? I bet any guy here would feel like a king if the smartest girl on campus asked him for help."

At his words, *I* feel like a king. "I'm not the smartest anymore."

"Bullshit."

I roll my eyes and fight a wide smile, unsuccessfully.

"You go up to Wade next class and ask him to tutor you, and watch what happens, Sand. I look forward to reading a full report."

But I shake my head. His instructions are not clear enough for one as socially inept as myself.

"In our thirteen years of friendship, have you ever seen me walk up to someone I'm not close to and initiate a conversation?" He ponders. "No, Jonny, you haven't. *How* do I ask him?"

"You're overthinking this with your big brain." He sets his cup down. "Practice on me. I'm Wade. Go."

I process his instructions. "Okay," I drawl. I straighten up in my chair. "Exc-c-use me."

"Sand. You don't need to be nervous. You're going to make this guy feel like Superman. Try, 'Hey, Wade,' instead." It's difficult not to melt into a puddle of love under the padded metal chair, even as he discusses my current crush. How can he know me so well, down to the consonants I prefer, and not *see* me? Not see what we could have?

How doesn't matter.

It's the reality, Sandra. He's not the one for you. Focus.

"Hey, Wade." My mind stalls.

"Damn, this guy must really be something. Just take a breath and say it. *Hey, Wade, I need help in this class. I was wondering if maybe you could tutor me?*"

I nod. "Hey, Wade, I need help in this class. I was wondering if maybe you could tutor me?"

"Good, but look up. It almost seems like you're asking but you don't really wanna ask. C'mon, Sand, let me see that perfect-SAT-score confidence."

I try a couple more times until Jonny is satisfied. Beyond satisfied, he's almost thrilled.

I try not to dwell on it. Maybe he knew he held my heart all this time and he's relieved I'm finally taking it back. Or maybe he's just enjoying the game of the experiment. Doesn't matter. He's helped, and quite a bit.

We talk for a half hour more, mostly about our families, our old acquaintances, and our new lives, his working full time and mine as a med student. He mentions Layla, too, but in a quick, guarded way. He assumes I'll never truly approve of her.

He is correct.

We part ways with another quick hug and a pair of wide smiles. I missed him so much.

"When does Wade get swept off of his feet?"

"Tomorrow."

"Awesome. I can't wait to read a detailed summary. I want it all, field notes, variables, constants, calculations, diagrams, slides, beakers—"

"Are you just listing all the scientific things you can think of?"

"Absolutely I am. I want all that in your email, k?" I nod. "Tomorrow, Sandy!" he calls as he leaves the cafe. I let myself stare at him as he goes.

CHAPTER 7

I can do this. I can do this. I can do this.

I slow my actions, methodically closing my laptop and notebook and returning them to my backpack. I slip my phone from my desk into my back pocket and grip my pen in my fingers. I rub my thumb up and down the hook on the side of the pen and count to ten.

When the commotion of departing students has died down, I begin my descent down the lecture hall stairs. I am amazed that my legs are functioning, as they are almost surely frozen. I wore my thinnest, cutest leggings today, with a cropped sweatshirt instead of a long warm one, per Avery's insistence. Wade sees me approach and offers a closed, polite smile. He maintains eye contact, and I curse Avery as my exposed ankles refuse to thaw.

"Sandra Hayes," he recalls playfully. I don't match his playful attitude, because I need to focus on the rehearsed words that are about to leave my mouth.

"Hey, Wade." Smile on my face—check. Eye contact—check. *So far so good!* "I need help with this class. Could you tutor me?" *Sweet victory!*

A dark lock of hair falls slightly out of place as he tilts his head. "I highly doubt that."

"I d-d-do," I sputter. I close my eyes for a second and take a small step back. *Deep breaths, that was barely noticeable.* When I reopen my eyes, Wade is looking at my legs. I'm almost certain. His eyes travel quickly up my body, heating my skin as they go. He clears his throat, as if guilty. As if he was caught being ungentlemanly.

This is good. He smiles, but I am frozen, unsure of what to do or say next. I need to extend my practice conversations!

"I'd be happy to help," he finally agrees. He grabs a sticky note stack from his messenger bag. "Do Tuesday evenings work for you? Or Thursdays?"

"Either." Such a lovely word without any hard consonants. He smiles and hands me the sticky note with a building and room number on it.

"Okay, tomorrow at seven."

I smile and nod and leave the room as quickly as possible. It's not a jog, because I would surely trip and make a fool of myself, but I move at a brisk pace, out of the room, out of the hall, and out of the building. On the sidewalk, I stop and breathe deeply.

I did it.

Sandy, it's 9pm. I know you had class with him today. How did it go???

Jonny,
He said, "I'd be happy to help," and we are meeting to-morrow night! I only slipped once but it was on the word

"do." You know how I hate that. It sounded like I was saying doo-doo. Ugh! He didn't seem bothered by it, but I froze up. I am considerably nervous about tomorrow. It was not decided explicitly that this was a date. It's not a date, is it? If it is a date, should I do anything differently than I would for a normal study session?
You did not adequately prepare me for this!
Sandy

Sand, you'll be fine! Just act as if it's a normal study session. I don't know what prodigies do on dates, but if it IS a date, I think you'll figure it out pretty quick ;) -J

I found room 401C in the library yesterday to alleviate at least one stressor for this evening. I'm wearing what Avery decided are my "lucky leggings" and a scented lotion. I also remembered to allow time for swapping my glasses for contacts and applying my new non-flaking mascara. I bought a tinted lip balm that I'm wearing as well. It is not sticky, smelly, or artificially flavored.

I feel good, ready. Not totally confident, but not anxious, either.

My intestines tighten as I near the room. I am exactly on time, which could mean I beat Wade here. That would surprise me, however, because most medical students I've met are as particular about punctuality and schedules as I am. I'm not inflexible, as I've been accused of, but rather just feel if a plan is made, it should be stuck to. As closely as possible for all parties. It's the considerate, logical way of behaving. I take a deep breath before I turn into the room.

I am surprised.

There are four people in the room.

Wade is one of them. "Sandra, you made it." He smiles warmly, and I feel myself blushing.

The two guys and one girl at the table don't look up. They are busy unpacking their notebooks. "Come on in," Wade adds, gesturing to the empty seat across from him.

So. This is a study *group.*

The two hours of study and discussion would have crawled by were it not for the interesting subject matter. I knew all of the material already, so I used the time for valuable review, quizzing myself in my mind. I answered if Wade asked me a specific question but otherwise quietly observed the scene. I found myself staring at Wade more than once. He is beautiful and intelligent. Very intelligent.

Finally, books are slamming shut and zippers are pulling closed.

Wade steps toward me slowly. "So, was it helpful?"

"Yeah, thanks," I say with a smile.

"Good." He smiles, too, and again, I'm frozen like an arachnid suddenly covered in shadow. "Well, have a good weekend?"

"Yeah!" I nod and start to make my way out the door. "You, too!"

> *Jonny,*
> *We need to meet for another lesson ASAP.*
> *S- everything ok??? - J*

> *Yes, everything is fine. But we need a new approach.*

Come to Sunday brunch?? - Jon

Sunday brunch.

I haven't been in years. I remember the food being delicious at the country club's formal open-seating brunch. A few neighborhood families, including mine and Jonny's, like to meet there at the same time. We didn't always get tables next to each other, but Jonny always insisted I sit next to him.

He put his arm around my chair once. He held my hand during a prayer on two different occasions. One Sunday, Rob accidentally burped aloud at the table, to the horror of his aunt and grandmother, and I couldn't stop laughing. Jonny whacked my exposed thigh under the table.

Even though I prefer one-on-one conversation, I didn't mind brunch. I used to look around the Canton table with such affection, imagining how it would be to bear the last name myself. I'd dream of our wedding reception in that very room. I imagined miniature Jonnies running around making Jon Senior laugh his too-loud bellow.

This would have to be a working Sunday brunch. Not a trip down memory lane or a time for dreaming and wishing. Just a meal with a friend, so he can help me seduce another man.

I can handle it.

Unless Layla will be there, with him.

Damn, I love this girl.

Love. And he'd said it right in front of me. Jonny's relationships were always a far-away idea. Even when I would see him and Layla in the halls of school, it was a quick glance at their joined hands. I've never had to witness him kiss her or see any affectionate touches.

I cannot handle that. Not yet.

Jonny, let's meet after for coffee just you and I instead. I'll be in town. - Sandy

Better. That'll be better.

CHAPTER 8

Jonny waves at me on his way to the counter. He's dressed in his Sunday Service clothes, a button-up shirt in a crisp, light blue shade, rolled to the elbow, with dark gray slacks. He lights up the whole mom-and-pop bakery, a much more comfortable spot than the campus cafe where we met last week.

Jonny sits down across from me in the squeaky booth with a huge, easy smile. His eyes look more blue and less aqua with that shirt.

He looks amazing.

I do not.

I lost track of time reading fiction this morning, as per my Sunday ritual, and was almost late due to suburban after-church traffic. Furthermore, I don't need to look amazing for Jonny. I need to look amazing for... Man, Jonny's eyes really look blue today...

WADE. His name is Wade, Sandra!

"Everything okay, Sandygirl? Your email had me worried."

He sounds like a brother, which is irritating. I sigh. "Yes, I'm fine."

"I still take boxing with my old football trainer Thad, you know. I can beat the guy up for you."

I relax. "Not necessary. He was fine. The problem was that it was most certainly *not* a date."

"It wasn't? Are you suuure, because—"

"There were three other students there."

Jonny deflates in his chair. "Oh. Well, that's a pretty dead give-away, then."

I give one firm nod before continuing. "So, our approach was not direct enough. And we need to extend our practice conversations further, beyond just two or three sentences."

"Got it. Okay. So you want to ask him flat-out on a date?"

"No! Absolutely not!"

"Why not?"

"Have you ever been asked out?"

He smiles like he's reliving his Star Quarterback Homecoming King days. "Most definitely."

"And did you say yes to any of those girls?"

His eyebrows knot. "No, I don't think I did." I cock my head at him. "Fair point, Doc. So? What now?"

"Alas. Gender roles live on. So I need to make it clear at the next study group that I don't want to study *with a group*. According to Lee and Avery, I need to flirt."

"Your old roommates, right?"

"Right."

He reaches a hand up and pulls on the back of his neck. "I dunno, Sand. How to flirt? I mean, you just do it. I'm not sure that can be taught. At least not by me, to a girl. What do they say, Lee and Avery?"

I glare at him. "Lee found a listicle online, and Avery sent me a few TikTok videos titled *How to Flirt.*"

"Oh, boy. Well. I can't believe this, but let's take a look at what Lee sent, I guess." I text him the link, and we both review the article together. "Yeah, standard stuff, eye contact, smiling, angling your body toward that person, yada, yada, yaaa... Okay. How about compliments? Want to practice that?"

I groan at him.

"Okay, then, Sandy, let's just shoot the shit and have coffee. I'm not the one on a mission here."

"Mission is an overstatement." He sends my own annoyed glare back at me. "All right...I like your shirt."

"Boooooooo!" He howls entirely too loudly.

My eyes bulge out of my head, and I slouch down in my chair. I forget sometimes how boisterous Jonny can be. He laughs at my discomfort.

"Sandy, that was pitiful. Now, look me in my eyes like I'm Wade and say something sweet."

I look up and stare straight into his eyes. I realize in that moment why I often look at his nose, or eyebrows, or his perfect straight, white teeth. Because his eyes are a trap for my consciousness. Every time. I let myself stare, just this once.

My voice is soft and scratchy when it emerges. "You might have the most beautiful eyes I've ever seen, likely that anyone has ever seen, in time's entirety."

"Nnnnice! He must be a real stunner, this dude. And! It all came out without a hitch. Just say exactly that."

I look down. It's moments like these that I'm certain of my situation. Lee asked me if maybe Jonny secretly loved me, too.

If he did, surely this would've been a moment. I could've sworn time slowed down, that he was going to have to slow blink and fight off a blush.

He thinks I was talking about Wade's eyes.

"Moving on!" I blurt loudly, feeling that familiar one-sided awkwardness. "What else?"

Jonny studies his phone before straightening up with new enthusiasm. "Ask personal questions. That'd be good to practice. Why don't you rattle off a few for him?"

"Hmm, okay." I sit up as well. "Have you chosen a specialty?"

"Good, dump them all out of your brain. And practice saying his name, too. 'Hey, Wade, have you chosen a specialty?"

I nod. He knows me well. "Hey, Wade, have you chosen a specialty? Hey, Wade, where are you from? Hey, Wade, where did you go for undergrad?"

"Easy-peasy, Sandygirl. You got those. Just go into your scientist mode like you're collecting data or whatever." He looks down at his phone again. "Now. You're not going to like this next one."

"Okay?" I wince.

He reads aloud, "Engage in small, unnecessary touches." He looks from his phone to me. "That is probably peak flirting. The most obvious of moves."

I shift backward in the booth. "Why wouldn't I like that?"

He flops his chin downward as he cocks one brow. "Sandy. Almost every time I've ever touched you since you were seven years old, you've frozen like a statue. Come on."

I slowly nod. He's right. I do freeze, but not for the reason he thinks. How could a guy so great with people be so oblivious with me? *Doesn't matter! Focus on the objective...whose name is WADE.*

"Maybe you don't have to initiate touching him, but try not to freeze when he touches you. Think you can handle that?"

"Yeah. I can. I think."

"Want to practice? I could grab your hand?"

"No!" I exclaim like I've been pinched under the table. I cannot take excessive touching from him right now. Not when I've been doing so well at shutting down all Jonny-related emotions. "No, thanks. I'll, uh, work my way up to that lesson."

Jonny gives me a small, understanding smile. Humorous, given he doesn't understand at all. He carries on, "K. Here's an easier one. Good one, too. Find a reason to give him your number."

"What kind of reason?"

"Hey, Wade," Jonny bats his lashes and talks in a breathy, high-pitched voice, "I can't make it to next class. Could you text me the chapters Professor So-and-So covers so I don't fall behind?"

"But I can always make it to class."

"So skip a class, Brainiac." I huff at him. "Or try the same tactic with study group, ask if he could text you what they covered."

"I suppose that could work."

He sets his phone down and levels me with a serious, focused look. I gulp. "I think we need to talk about your recovery." I have no idea what he means. "You said you froze after you said doo-doo."

"Jonny!" He lifts his hand in surrender with a smile as I die. *Cause of death: extreme mortification.*

"You know I'm right! You're gonna get nervous, you're gonna flub it up a bit, and you can't let that get you down. It's not a big deal."

I squint at him. "You'll be shocked to learn there has been minimal flubbing for over two years. Many of my classmates in undergrad had no idea."

"I'm not shocked at all. I never doubted your ability to master it. To master *anything.* I just thought you may, possibly, in some teeny tiny nervous part of you, want to at least discuss a post-doo-doo response plan."

"Hmmmm. What do you propose?"

He takes a triumphant sip of his coffee. After a beat, his face lights up. "I've got it. Tell him he makes you nervous."

"What!"

"It's perfect. It tells him you like him, it'll make him feel important, and, *and* Sandy—this is perfect—you can even use it as an opportunity to make a joke, like, 'You know what, from now on let's just talk to each other by text. Let me give you my number so we can continue this conversation.'"

He leans back and waggles his eyebrows. For a second, he's ten years old again, and a connection to the visual in my brain makes the edges of my ribcage hurt. I shrug away the feeling. "It's not the *worst* response plan I've ever heard."

"I'm starting to wonder who the genius is here. In a few days, you will be texting this guy non-stop, getting ready for your first date."

The idea of a date floods my system with cortisol. I tense up and shake my head. "You know what? This is dumb. I already asked him to tutor me. If he was interested, he would've asked me out by now."

"No, Sandy, trust me, some guys can be really oblivious." *You don't say.*

"And asking him to tutor me when I probably have the highest grade in the class, that wasn't obvious enough?"

"Nope. Trust me, as soon as he realizes you're actually flirting and not just trying to get a higher grade or just being polite or whatever, he'll be pumped. He'll ask you for your number right away if he's not too chicken. What guy wouldn't want to date the smartest girl in the class?"

You. You wouldn't. "Maybe."

"Absolutely, Sand, not maybe. Now. Say doo-doo ten times and then recover."

"Jonny, I am not—"

"Doo doo! Doo doo! Doo doo!" He gets louder. A little old lady two tables over gives us the side-eye.

I lean in to whisper-scream, "Are you five years old?! Stop it!"

He matches my tone and leans in as well. "No, I'm helping you!"

"Fine!"

"Fine!" He leans back in anticipation.

"You really are a good friend for helping me with this, Jonny."

"The best. I am the *best* friend."

"Yeah. You are."

And that's all you'll ever be.

The thought prompts me to focus on the task—all right, the *mission*—at hand. I complete all of Jonny's ridiculous speech exercises, during which both of us dissolve into delirious laughter. The little old lady eventually gets up and relocates to a table on the other side of the space. Jonny is always quick to laugh, but I never laugh like this with anyone other than him. I've come close with Lee and Avery before, but not quite.

Could Wade make me laugh so hard my eyes water? Could he be the second person to make me snort-laugh my latte?

I'm surprised when I realize I am genuinely excited to find out.

CHAPTER 9

Lucky leggings squeezing around my thighs, and in need of a launder, I am ready to flirt with Wade after class. But Wade is absent, leaving me cold and disappointed. At least I was completely enthralled with a lecture from our actual professor. I even forgot about the discomfort in my extremities.

Thursday evening, I set multiple alarms for myself, making sure I arrive at room 401C early enough to talk to Wade before the group session begins. As I near the room, I wonder if we are having the session at all, since it's possible Wade could be sick or out of town. I slow my steps, considering this. If I had his number, I would be able to text him to ask if we were still meeting.

What a lucky turn of events!

I enter the room to find that Wade is indeed there, with Joel, one of the other participants. I walk directly to Wade and begin talking before I lose my nerve.

"I wasn't sure we were meeting."

"Hey, Sandra—"

"If I had your number, I could've texted you to ask if the session was still on for tonight." I look at him, forcing myself to maintain eye contact. He looks confused. I try to smile, to show that I am, indeed, flirting, but his scowl only deepens. It's possible my smile is presenting as more of a wince or a cringe. *Crap! Relax, face! Relax!* I sigh and look down.

"Sure, uh, sorry I didn't think of that last week. Here." He hands me his phone, open to the Add New Contact screen, without hesitation. This is promising. I input my information quickly and hand his phone back to him. My hands betray me, shaking like two liquids in the chem lab's oscillator. I sit quickly and begin busying them with the removal of the contents of my bag.

The study session passes slowly and without any Wade-related progress. I try to angle myself toward him, mimic his body language with my own, and make eye contact. He does not seem to notice or react to any of my signals. As practiced in class, I slow my actions when the session concludes. It's almost painful to pull a zipper this slowly!

My throat is completely clogged when we are left alone in the small room. Wade waits for me by the door with all of his forehead's Frontalis muscles in a twist.

I stop in front of him and make eye contact.

Compliment him!

"Everything okay?" Wade asks. I can't seem to get the words to my throat, which means they definitely won't escape my mouth catch-free. "...Sandra?"

"You look like a vampire!"

Wade recoils slightly.

I continue too loudly, "No! I mean the hot one, you kn-n-now, Ian Somerhalder but lessss b-b-b-roody."

He finally starts to grin. "Thank you?"

I squeeze my eyes shut and nod, feeling like my ten-year-old self, in a bright classroom surrounded by sneering giggles.

"Hey," Wade puts a tentative hand on my shoulder, "I haven't watched his show, but my sister always went on and on about him." I can hear from the sounds of his voice that he is smiling as he speaks. I still can't open my eyes.

"You make me nervous," I whisper. I open my eyes after my confession and am met with his stunning smile. I have to look away as I feel every nerve ending in the epidermis of my face start to tingle.

He's genuinely surprised. "I do?" I nod. "Sooo you didn't really need a tutor," he says, and I transition the nod to a firm shake. His smile grows. "I'm glad."

I finally look back up, directly into his eyes. They're not the entirety of the ocean captured in a pair of irises, but they are consuming in their own way. He squeezes the hand that's still on my shoulder three times, and warmth floods all my internal systems.

"Want to go get something to eat? Coffee? Dessert or something?"

My smile starts to match his.

"Sssssssure."

"Don't be nervous, Sandra. I think you're incredible." With that earth-tilting admission, said so plainly, he gestures toward the door with his head. He leads me out of the library before I can respond.

We don't chat on the short walk from the library to the small dessert bar nearby. I do catch Wade looking down at me a couple times. I sneak glances up at him in return. He's absolutely gorgeous. And quiet. It's different but comfortable, walking together in silence. I usually walk in silence alone, but his warmth on my right is a welcome sensation.

We sit with our ice cream—two hot fudge sundaes, mine without nuts or cherries—and I prepare myself for small talk. Luckily, I practiced these questions. And, to my surprise, Wade has plenty of questions about me that he claims he's wondered since our first day of class.

He knows from our professor that I graduated from both high school and college early. He tells me he graduated from college a year early himself. It feels as if we are part of a very small sub-community within med school.

At learning this, for the first time maybe ever, I don't feel like a complete outsider. Even with Lee and Avery, I was younger than both of them, yet we all knew from the start I'd graduate before they did. They accepted me and loved me, of course, but even as a member of our happy threesome, I was set apart.

I barely realize that I've easily asked him a whole host of un-rehearsed questions and have answered many from him as well. The lights behind the counter of the little shop go dark, signaling we've been talking for over an hour. They also urge us politely to promptly vacate the store. We do.

We walk slowly back to the library where my car is parked. Once we reach the sidewalk entrance to the library lot, we pause together, instinctually.

"I'm glad you called me a vampire tonight." Wade chuckles, a cute half-laugh, and I groan. "C'mon, admit it, it'll be a hilarious story for us to tell everyone at parties. How the gorgeous girl genius Dr. Sandra Hayes seduced me with insults at the library."

"Seduced!" I squeak.

His eyes barely squint, and his voice lowers in response. "An accurate categorization."

The depth of his voice and seriousness of his gaze affect me like his shoulder squeeze earlier. No one has ever looked at me this way before. He moves closer to me, and I feel all of my limbs tense without my permission. He's going to kiss me. *Isn't he? I am not very well-versed at this! What if I have chocolate on my lips? Are my lips chapped? I have not been maintaining my night-time Chapstick routine!*

He hesitates for a moment, and then I find his arms firmly wrapped around me. After a millisecond, I return the embrace. All the long hugs of my life thus far have been with either my mother or Jonny. Wade is taller than Jonny but not as bulky or as warm. He smells like the woods and oranges and soap. My thoughts about my sensory perception of him—*not* in relation to Jonny but just in general—are still forming when his long, muscular arms are suddenly gone.

He clears his throat. "I'll text you?"

"Uh huh," I say as he smiles wide and turns to walk away.

He didn't kiss me.

Why didn't he kiss me?

Did I want him to kiss me?

I can't decide if I am disappointed or relieved before I hear my favorite sound.

Sandy! Mission Status Report STAT! I know tonight was your study session! - J

Jonny,

Operational success. I embarrassed myself and called him a vampire, but he still asked me to have ice cream. He also graduated early from undergrad, like me. He is also interested in orthopedics and also neurology. I managed to give him my number. Overall, I relied on our lessons and the listicle, and I would say these are some very positive results! - Sandy

---

A whizkid like you! Sounds perfect. Now you can text him! Please make sure he understands that you will be having a best man at the wedding, not a maid of honor. This is important. - J

Jonny! He just texted me! We have not covered flirting over text! Please advise ASAP!

My phone buzzes again, after having just alerted me to Wade's message asking if I made it home all right and the email chimes from Jonny. It is a lot of stimulation. I consider putting the annoying device on airplane mode.

Jonny: Permission to transfer our conversation from email to text?

Me: Granted.

Jonny: Step one: remain calm.

Jonny: I know you're more than capable of blocking out notifications.

Jonny: Take your time.

Jonny: Just because he messages you doesn't mean to reply right away.

I sit and stare at the little screen. I am having a text conversation with Jonny. We've hardly texted and never conversed at length before. It buzzes again.

Jonny: ...I mean when HE messages you.

Jonny: For ME, you reply right away!

Me: Noted. I am processing all of this.

Jonny: Do you want to talk on the phone instead?

Me: What do you think?

Jonny: LOL Just a joke!

Jonny: I know you hate the phone. ;)

Jonny: So what did he text you?

Me: He said, "Did you make it home all right?"

Jonny: Did you?

Me: Yes.

Jonny: I still think it'd be safer for you to live with roommates than in an apartment alone...

Me: I wanted to live with my parents and commute, but they insisted I was too young to "become a spinster homebody with no social life."

Jonny: Eh, spinster life suits you.

Me: What?!

Jonny: Are you drinking tea under a quilt right now or not?

Jonny: ...

Jonny: HA! All that's missing is a few cats.

Jonny: Which I bet you would already have if you didn't have to study so much.

Jonny: Right?

Jonny: RIGHT?

Jonny: Sandy?

Jonny: I'm sorry you're not a spinster. You'll never be one, either. You'll be a superstar genius giving people new hips and bionic knees.

Me: Please refrain from sending so many short messages at once. I had to go over this with Avery. Gather your thoughts and then send one long message.

Jonny: Noted. Did you reply to him?

Me: No, I was busy being teased.

Jonny: Suck it up, buttercup. You know you're my favorite nerdy old soul who drinks tea and likes quilts and old hardback novels. Also, I just remembered your cat allergy, so I take that part back. Now. Just say, "Yes, thanks for asking," with a smiley.

Me: OK.

Me: Yes, thanks for asking. =)

Wade: Of course.

Wade: Do you have any big plans this weekend?

Me: He's asking if I have plans this weekend.

Jonny: He clearly doesn't know you very well yet. Just reply no— even though YOU think studying 24/7 counts as plans, it doesn't!

Me: [glare emoji]

Me: Just studying.

Wade: Think you could take a dinner break on Saturday?

Me: !!!! He said, "Think you could take a dinner break on Saturday?" PLEASE ADVISE! IS HE ASKING ME OUT?

Jonny: Sand, please don't shout at me electronically. How rude.

Me: Sorry.

Jonny: I'm KIDDING! DEEP BREATHS! Yes, he is asking you out. Looks like Dr.Nerd has some cahones after all, good for him.

Me: What do I say?

Jonny: Do you want to go on a second date?

Me: Second date?

Jonny: Ice cream counted as date number one.

I put my phone down for a moment. I'm trembling, and I'm not sure if it's because Wade is asking me out or Jonny is texting with me after eleven p.m. So many nights I've wanted to text Jonny to say hello and simply ask how he was, where he was, what he was doing. But the door to this method of communication had never been opened. Now it has, and I'm concerned it may as well have been Pandora's Box.

Focus, Sandra! And not on Jonny! Who is with Layla! Do I want a second date with Wade?

Me: Yes, I want a second date.

Jonny: Then say yes, silly. Again, who is the genius here?

Me: [Animate Gif: Shitts Creek: David Rolling His Eyes]

Me: Yes, I will need to stop and eat dinner.

Wade: Sustenance is vital for optimal information retention.

Me: Precisely.

Wade: Can I take you out for said sustenance break?

Me: Yes.

Wade: Excellent. Do you have any dietary restrictions?

Me: No.

Wade: Pick you up at seven?

Me: OK.

Jonny: So? What did you say?

Me: [Screenshot]

Jonny: ...you do like this guy, right?

Me: Correct.

Jonny: Doesn't look like it, Sand. Give the poor guy some hope—maybe throw in an exclamation point or two? A smiley face or a heart or something?

Me: It's too late now! You should've told me that before!!!!!

Jonny: Oh, look, now she's got punctuation marks.

Me: HELP!!!!!!!!!!!!!!!

Jonny: Say, "Sounds great!"

Me: OK. Sent.

Jonny: All right, now put your phone on silent and go read something before all that tension in your shoulder muscles snaps and your head just up and falls off.

Me: LOL you don't know how our bodies work. You do know me, however. I am tense.

Jonny: Right, so get outta here. Nite, Sandy.

Me: Good night.

I try to read, but my mind is tired and muddled with feelings. So many feelings. Eventually, I fall asleep with a huge smile on my face. I'm just not entirely sure which text conversation put it here.

CHAPTER 10

Me: I chickened out on the date.

Jonny: WHAT!

Jonny: Did something happen?

Jonny: Are you all right?

Jonny: Sand????

Jonny: Sorry. Too many texts at once.

Me: Like the Sandy Cuts Her Own Bangs Tragedy of seven years ago, this is one of those instances where I need you to agree NOT to laugh and/or tease me. Since I cannot see you, the laughter is optional. The prohibition of teasing is not.

Jonny: If you did cut your own bangs again, can we FaceTime?

Me: I did not, and no, we cannot. Do you agree?

Jonny: Agreed.

Me: The thing is, I have never been on a real date.

Jonny: What?

Me: Feel free to re-read what I sent as many times as is necessary to fully understand my predicament.

Jonny: You're twenty! That just can't be true. What about Winter formal? Prom?

Me: Winter formal I went with a group. I didn't go to prom.

Jonny: Wow.

Jonny: Still, you went with him for ice cream.

Me: There was no picking up, no fancy dinner, no dropping off. I got so worked up this morning I just grabbed my phone and texted him that I was unwell. He said, "Rain check?" and I said, "Definitely!" With the !

Jonny: Okay. Well, I hope you're sitting down for this but...you're over-thinking things.

Me: [unimpressed emoji]

Jonny: Seriously, it's exactly like ice cream just with different food and a slight change of transportation to and from.

Me: Then why does it feel completely different?

Jonny: Because you're crazy?

Me: Per our agreement established after the Bangs Incident, you owe me $25.

Jonny: That was considered teasing?!

Me: Without question.

Jonny: Then I'm sorry and I'll pay you when I see you.

Jonny: When is the make-up date and how can we get you ready?

Me: I'll never be ready. I'm hopeless.

Jonny: Wow, Code Black, huh?

Jonny: So you were supposed to go out with him tonight... Do you want to do a practice run instead?

Me: What does practice run mean?

Jonny: I'll take you on a practice date tonight. Pick you up, take you to dinner, drop you off at home. You'll see it's just a normal meal.

Me: It's a Saturday night. You don't have plans?

Jonny: Layla's out of town for work. Come on, it'll be fun.

Me: OK.

Jonny: I'm already headed to the city. Pick you up at seven?

Me: OK.

Jonny: Send me the address. Is it The Willows or that other complex to the South?

Me: [address]

I tell myself to remain calm. I remind all my body's systems that when Jonny arrives at my door any second now, it's not a real date. Jonny is dating Layla. Jonny *loves* Layla. And I like Wade. He is what all of this is for. *Wade, Wade, Wade, Wade.*

There's a knock on the door. *Jonny.*

I open the door, and I immediately regret all of the life choices that have led me to this moment. This moment where Jonny Canton is dressed up in a suit jacket and jeans, with a teal shirt—a teal shirt!—and holding a small bouquet of daises, looking like he walked directly out of my dreams.

But it's not real.

But it also *is* real.

I shudder, knowing tonight is sure to be a Knife Email, disguised as a training exercise with my best friend.

"Teal," is what my brain manages to summon from my consciousness and push through my mouth. Not, "Hi," "Hey," or "Hello," but "Teal."

"When I was sixteen, you told me I should wear teal every single day of my life."

I nod at the memory, but I don't reopen my mouth.

Jonny hicks up one shoulder as he offers me the flowers. "Layla likes daises. So."

Stab number one.

"Thank you." I turn to set them on the entry credenza, eager to look away from his perfect face.

"Hey." He sounds unusually serious, so I quickly look back at him. "Where are your glasses?"

"Oh, right. I overcame my fear of contacts, finally, a while ago."

"Huh." He is staring at me, like he used to do when we were kids, if I'd just said something about Pythagorean's theorem or metacarpal bones. We both appear to be frozen.

"Do you—shhhhould I invite *him* in?"

Jonny shakes himself out of his stupor. "Well, you're already wearing your parka fit for the arctic, so it might be a bit weird. You seem ready to go, plus, if he's made a reservation, you won't want to dilly-dally around and be late anyway. You could offer just a quick once-over."

"Well, that's easy." I gesture wide with my hand. "It's a one-bedroom apartment. You've already seen most of it."

He glances around. "It's nice."

"You're lying."

He rolls his eyes. "It's a pre-furnished apartment you're clearly never in, Sand. It's fine."

My shoulders sag. "Avery did most of the decorating in my last place."

"Come on, Doc, he's not dating your apartment. He's dating you. Who cares?" He heads back through to apartment and opens it. "Plus, I *did* make a reservation, so I'll have to complete the tour after dinner."

"You did?"

"Of course." He motions forward, holding the door open for me. "It's your first real date. Where'd you think I was going to take you, Applebees?"

I turn around to lock my door, shaking my head, hoping all my worrisome emotions fall out. *Not real, Sandra. Not real!* "That's very thoughtful of you, but this isn't my first real date. This is practice."

I retrieve my key and face him, finding the same confused stare, like he's never seen me before. "Right. Sorry. Definitely not a real date." Jonny starts walking, and I follow. "But if Dr. Dorkus is worth all this fuss, he'll take you someplace fancy."

"He's not a dork, you know."

Those teal eyes squint back at me over Jonny's shoulder. "Suuuuure he's not."

I roll my eyes with a huff, and Jonny laughs.

"Reservation for Canton." Jonny beams his megawatt smile at the hostess. Becca, according to her gold name tag, loses her breath at the sight of him and almost trips in her excitement to walk him to his table. Unclear at this time if she knows I am also part of his reservation.

The Steakhouse, a very fancy, old-money, reservations-required restaurant, is packed. And, surprisingly, not just with fancy old people. Jonny waves at multiple people on our walk to the table. One man stops Jonny and shakes his hand with a greeting. That's the life of a Canton in both Oklahoma City and Tulsa and even Dallas. He doesn't mind it, and I'm used to it. Little Becca's face, however, looks as if she's escorting a Kardashian in the flesh. We eventually arrive at our absolutely-not-romantic candlelit corner table.

"Here, let's let her take our coats back to the front, Sand," Jonny says as he reaches to help me, which dashes all of Becca's hopes and dreams. I shrug out of my puffer coat with a smile. I know it's overkill for winter in Oklahoma, but I loathe being cold.

"Thanks," I say brightly, enjoying Becca's turmoil much more than I should. But my smile disappears when I see Jonny grimacing at me. It looks as if the musculature of his face might actually be in pain.

I am grossly under-dressed for this restaurant.

Avery chose my tight black jeans and a slouchy mustard shirt that is a mixture between a sweatshirt and a sweater. It falls off one shoulder in a way that bothers me, but she insisted I take it from her closet and keep it years ago because she "couldn't pull off the color." She also insisted I wear it on my date with Wade, which she does not yet know was canceled this evening. I need to stop letting her make my wardrobe choices, clearly.

I whisper loudly as my eyes dart around. "Uh, sorry, I only thought about the cold. I should've worn a dress."

Jonny shakes the disgust off of his face and shoves our coats at Becca without even glancing in her direction. His voice is unusually scratchy. "Nah, there's no such thing as a dress code at these places anymore. Wait." He stops me from pulling out my chair. His voice recovers. "Let me, my lady."

"My l—"

"Don't even try to tease me, Einstein. Class is officially in session." He huffs as he pushes my chair in and then continues as he takes his seat across from me. "Let Whatshisname pull your chair out for you and be chill about it." I bite my lip to keep from laughing or calling him sir or breaking out my absurd British accent.

"His name is Wade and you know it."

His eyes sparkle in the candlelight around us, and I find it difficult not to stare. *Look away, Sandra! This is not real!*

Jonny looks down at the menu, breaking our connection that he probably didn't feel as strongly as I did anyway. "You still only eat red meat about once a month?"

I smile and feel my eyebrows raise in surprise at his memory. "Roughly."

"Trust me, you're gonna want tonight to be the night. They didn't name this place The Steakhouse for nothing." I give him a skeptical look. "Steak and potatoes and salad with ranch. Welcome back to the heartland, baby."

It takes a considerable amount of time to recover from that last word. I remind myself Jonny jokes. It's what he does. He has said baby in that same tone a million times before; it means nothing.

We talk as easily over dinner as we did over coffee. Jonny carries the conversation with hilarious stories and self-deprecating jokes. He asks me a few questions about my college experience, quickly deciding I did way too much studying and not nearly enough partying. He asks about med school, but he gets that glazed-over look on his face, so I don't go into much detail.

Instead of changing the subject, though, he seems almost reverent. "Suma Cum Laude at Stanford in three years, Sand." He shakes his head in disbelief. The sincerity of it, the admiration from him, makes my skin flush a deep crimson color. "Hey!" I look up, and his eyes are wide. "Did you just move your foot under the table?"

I did. His shoe had found my boot, and I quickly moved it away.

"Sandy, if you like this guy, let him play some innocent footsie with you. Put your foot back where it was."

"You're ridiculous."

"I'm docking your grade, Miss Hayes."

I find my foot with his. "Wait, you came up with a grading system?"

"I knew that would work!" He laughs too loudly. "Now keep your foot there a while, even though you hate it. This is good practice."

He moves both his feet around mine under the table. In fact, I can feel his calves touching mine. I don't mind. I don't hate it at all.

A man about Jonny's dad's age comes up and stands at the side of our table, chatting away about Jon Senior and golf and the business, seemingly totally unaware of his surroundings. Jonny politely dismisses him with a comment that he doesn't want to bore his lovely date.

That's me.

He just said I was his lovely date.

Before I can swoon too hard internally, his face grows somber. He leans in and whispers, more serious than I've seen him in years. "Sandy. Be completely honest here..." I swallow as he looks around us and then back into my eyes. "Did Mr. Langston just crop dust us?! Tell me you smell that!"

I burst out laughing with relief as Jonny sniffs dramatically before laughing with me.

My fit of giggles finally subsides with a sigh. "You are a child."

We laugh through dessert and the drive home. He makes me suffer through two awful pop songs, "in case Dr. Dweeb has crap taste in music." He asks about my upcoming week and if I'm nervous about any looming tests. Then we're parked on the street of my complex.

He shifts his bulky body toward me. "Remember, don't just hop out of the car. Let him come around and get the door for you."

"I knoooow!"

"Do you? Because earlier you opened your own car door, then restaurant door, and then you almost pulled out your own chair. You're lucky I'm not deeply offended."

I cock my head. "Wait, what if I forget? Do you think he might really be offended by that?"

His face relaxes into what I'd describe as absolute warmth. His voice is soft as he clarifies. "No, Sandy. Not really." I watch him hustle around to get my door for me. I climb out, and we move to the sidewalk. He clears his throat and reverts to his stern teacher voice. "Now, if this were a real date, I'd make a move to hold your hand on our walk to the door."

Jonny shifts me to the inside of the sidewalk using his right hand on my right bicep. Before I even realize it, he's slipped his left hand into my right as he moves, all in one smooth motion.

Jonny is holding my hand.

I'm holding hands with Jonny.

I...

He...

We're...

I...

Jonny says something.

"What?"

"I said I had fun tonight, Sandy. I missed this. I hated being a thousand miles apart."

One thousand six hundred miles.

"I know it was more than a thousand miles. Whatever it was, it was too far for me."

"Me too."

We've already arrived the steps that lead up to my apartment unit. Jonny turns and takes both of my hands in his and turns to face me. A fire breaks out in both my palms and quickly engulfs my whole body. He tenses, feeling my reaction, and confusion flashes across his face before he lets go and takes a step back.

"So." He's loud all of a sudden. "He, uh, he could kiss you right here or he may pause and stand here hoping that you invite him up, but I didn't realize how late it is. I can't come up and help you with that part, and you decide if you're ready for what that means, you know, him coming up. It doesn't have to mean anything, either. You can just kiss him here and that can be it. Or you can not kiss him at all, either."

Is Jonny rambling?

"But anyway, whatever you decide, now you see this was just like any other dinner, nothing to be nervous about, kiddo."

Kiddo. Stab number two.

"Layla's flight just landed. I didn't realize it was so late. She'll kill me if she's just standing there on the curb, you know? Luckily I stopped earlier to get her flowers, and yours, too, so I don't have to stop on the way to the airport."

Stab number three.

"Right," I croak out.

He starts to walk away and calls back, "Night, Sandy! Text me before the big date—the real one!"

The real one.

He's right.

I need to focus on the real date.

Well, aside from focusing on school, obviously, which is still overwhelming and some days even terrifying. That's plenty of mental load for me right now.

School, weekly chats with my parents, weekly FaceTime with Lee and Avery, and sweet, smart, handsome Wade.

Nothing else.

No one else.

CHAPTER 11

It seems Pandora's Box was indeed opened, because over the past two weeks since our fake date, Jonny has texted me multiple times a day. I've had to turn my phone on silent—not vibrate, but silent—so I can think.

I should've expected this behavior. After all, Jonny always has a lot to say. He sends memes, takes selfies, takes photos of things he thinks I'll find interesting or funny. One day, during a visit in the Texas panhandle to scout locations for a new Canton Cards store, he went on a trek through a nearby field just to find interesting bugs to show me.

I loved it.

I was frustrated and lonely at the library, and his texts changed my entire day. Still, I wince even now, knowing his texts shouldn't influence my mood the way they do. Where is all that mental toughness?

Tonight is my actual first date with Wade. I braced myself for a barrage of instructions and reminders, yet suddenly my phone has gone still. It's possible Jonny is flying home from a meeting. It's Saturday, so he might be hanging with Layla. He probably is.

And I'm about to go out on my first ever real date, with a hot fourth-year med student! *Focus, Sandra!*

After my anxiety-induced delay, Wade got the flu. My classes are so intense, I've barely minded the wait. Plus, Wade is as adept at texting as Jonny. He sends med school jokes, orthopedics memes, and occasionally sweet notes like, "I can't wait for our date," or, "I missed seeing you this week."

Avery and Lee are so excited I wonder if they might be falling in love with Wade themselves. Avery ordered me a new warm-yet-sexy shirt to go with the tight, light-wash jeans we all agreed looked best over FaceTime. Lee sent four articles with titles such as "Acing Your First Date." They were informative.

I'm nervous, but not terribly so. Wade has put me at ease with his texts. We're going to a nice restaurant that he described as quiet but not fancy. He sent a link to the menu and an address for a trendy hot chocolate bar near the restaurant. An hour ago, he messaged me, "I'm excited to see you in an hour, Gorgeous Girl Genius!"

Exactly one hour later, I'm opening my door. My breath catches at the sight of him, clean shaven, in a gray sweater over a white shirt with dark jeans, holding a small bouquet of glaringly bright roses.

"Hi," he smiles tentatively. I catch him looking down at the deep V-neck of my shirt, filled out by a brand new push-up bra, and quickly looking back to my eyes. He extends the flowers. "I almost went with the classic red, but you said your favorite color was teal. They're dyed, but it turns out there aren't any naturally teal flowers. That I could find, anyway."

Teal. I blink at them for a few moments, kicking myself for inviting Jonny into this evening before it has even started.

"You hate that they're dyed, don't you?" Wade starts to slump a bit.

"No! Not at all. I just didn't know what to say." He straightens back up with a smile. I smile back. "That was very thoughtful, thank you." I finally take the flowers from his hand and, in a move I read online, turn away but call over my shoulder. "I will put these in some water. Please, c-c-come in."

"No roommates?" His eyebrows lift as he steps in. I watch him from the kitchen sink, which is in the bar that opens into the tiny living space and dining nook. The apartment is modern and open, with just one short hall for my utility closet door and bedroom door.

"I didn't know anyone yet." He nods, looking around the sparse space. "It came furnished and decorated, and I haven't bothered to change anything, since I'm not here much."

"Oh, I get it. I have two roommates I never see and our apartment came empty and is still mostly empty. This place is great." I relax as I turn off the water and push the vase to the corner of the bar. The little display adds a significant amount of cheer.

I gesture toward the hall behind him. "I have my own washer and dryer there, and just one bedroom. And bathroom, obviously." I walk around back into the entry area that is also the living area, where he stands. He takes up a lot of space in my tiny home. I like it. I like the look of him standing there. I'm unsure of what to do next, causing my pulse rate to increase rapidly.

"Shall we?" he asks, taking charge. I grab my coat and lead him out. I lock my door and feel a whisper of deja vu. Except when I turn around, Wade doesn't look at me like he's confused, or like I'm a kid sister, or like he's about to make a joke. His stare is intense and his closed smile is tight. He vaguely reminds me of a hungry jaguar I watched track an antelope on a Netflix special last week.

My insides clench as my cheeks heat. Is Wade going to pounce on me like a predator? Do I want him to?

I think I do.

But he gestures for me to lead the way, and we go to his car. He does open the door for me. He does not have terrible music playing in his car. He puts his hand on the small of my back as we walk through the restaurant. I've read about that move in novels and in articles Lee sent. It's a *distinct sign of attraction and possessiveness.* No one has ever put their hand there before.

I like it.

Wade takes my coat, and then we sit and peruse the menu. He confirms that I'm not yet twenty-one and refrains from ordering wine for us. Then, as if he knows the server will interrupt us anyway, he waits. He doesn't jump to fill the silence. I don't, either. And neither of us is uncomfortable by this. It's nice.

After ordering, we talk easily about first-date things. We cover our childhoods, our parents and siblings, and our favorite subjects within medicine. His feet come around mine under the table, and I am able to fight my instinct to pull away. It makes me think of Jonny, of course, but I refocus with a question for Wade about my professor whom he assists.

The dinner is completely hitch-free, until it isn't.

"So, past boyfriends? Any heartbreakers?"

I choke on my water at these questions. I find it embarrassing that the answer is no, no boyfriends, even though I am twenty years old and have completed both high school and college. Furthermore, yes, there has been a heartbreaker, over and over again, and we never even dated! Humiliating!

Wade leans in and reaches a hand in my direction. "We don't have to get into all that yet if you don't want to."

I shake my head. "There hasn't been anyone noteworthy." I realize that it's a lie after it slips from my lips.

"Really?" His shock at my answer increases my unease. I should've dated. I should've had boyfriends. I should've done a lot of things. I gulp down the emotions and redirect my thought patterns.

"What about you?" I ask.

"Noteworthy, huh? I guess there were a couple. I dated a girl in high school for two years. Young love and all that. We grew apart after graduation, but it was amicable. Then another serious relationship in undergrad. We wanted different things."

I nod. I want to ask what different things he means. What does he want? But then, what do I want? Do I know what I want? I know I want to be a leading orthopedic surgeon. Beyond that, all the things I've ever wanted were specific... the church wedding, a couple of little boys with teal eyes, a house with its very own tornado shelter...

"Sandra?"

"Sorry. What was that?"

"The hot chocolate place? Do you want to try it?"

"Yes. Yes, I want to try it. With you."

It's a short, frigid walk to the trendy beverage bar. Wade apologizes for not driving and puts his arm around me. He smells lovely.

We chat easily over dessert, talking about our favorite books, movies, and music. He doesn't read much fiction, but I can't hold that against him. Between his coursework, his TA classes, and the study groups he facilitates, it sounds like his schedule is, as Avery would say, Totally Batshit.

Hearing him describe his upcoming week as we stand up to leave has me concerned. "When do you eat? Sleep? Exercise?"

He cocks his head at me. "Exercise?"

"You clearly do something regularly to maintain," I gesture up and down toward him, "this."

His eyes light up like a jaguar again. "Dr. Hayes, are you saying you appreciate my runner's *anatomy*?"

I roll my own. "It was merely a scientific observation, Dr. Anderson."

"Oh, right, of course." He smirks as he opens the door for me.

"I also run. I find it meditative, as well as effective for cardiovascular health, of course," I say, trying to move on from the topic of my attraction to him.

"It's effective for you in more ways than one, Sandra." He grabs my hand and interlocks our fingers. I like this move, and my face tingles. But I also notice that my whole body does not combust in response to this. And my hands are a bit clammy. And sticky! There was chocolate residue on the outside of my cup. *Dammit! No one likes for their hands to be sticky!*

My body tenses, and Wade looks down at me. He lets go of my hand and puts an arm around me instead, saying something about the cold that I can't hear. My ears are filled with the whooshing sound of my pulse. My ears must be a deep red due to the blood flow of embarrassment.

118

In the car, he turns the heat up to maximum velocity and connects my phone to his sound system. I show him a few tracks that demonstrate why oldies music is better than current pop. Then I choose a couple tracks to explain how Tchaikovsky offers so much more than "just that Christmas ballet song." He demands that I balance these opinions by defending my position on country music. I go with "Friends in Low Places."

"Really? That's the best song country has to offer?" he asks as he puts the car in park and turns the ignition.

"No, but it's a happy one, and I predict you will find this song playing in your head later tonight, and tomorrow, and the next time you get a little drunk with your roommates."

"Hm," he mumbles, and he gets out, and I get out, too, forgetting the rules. Wade doesn't seem to mind. Instead he takes my hand again for the short walk to my steps.

I quickly think through the options Jonny rattled off. Is this the end of the date? Do I invite him up? Do I wait for him to imply he *wants* me to invite him up? If he comes up, what do I want to happen up there?

But Wade quickly wraps me in a tight embrace that squeezes the questions from my head. He pulls back and looks down at me like a man starved would look at a piece of steak just removed from the grill. I inhale sharply, trying to remember the status of my lips and my breath.

Wade smiles and pulls me into him using the zipper of my coat, which is not pulled all the way to the top. He pulls it up to my neck and hugs me again. I feel his hot breath on my ear. Goose bumps erupt at every hair follicle on my skin. Every single one.

"Don't wear that shirt to class." He kisses me just outside of my ear and then on my cheek, and just as I close my eyes for a real kiss, he lets me go.

I open my eyes, and he smiles at me as he backs away and whispers, "Good night, gorgeous."

I can feel the "g" stuck in my throat so I just wave.

That's twice he didn't kiss me.

Am I unkissable?

I need to determine the answer to this question as soon as possible, *without* involving the one person I most want to ask.

CHAPTER 12

"You are NOT unkissable! You were probably visibly nervous last night. Were you? Were you agitated?" Lee asks in between bites. I hold the phone back up so she can see my face.

"Lee. How do I know if I was visibly agitated or not? I could not see myself!"

"Orkr, but do you *fthink* you were?"

"Lee. The chewing. We've discussed this." She mutes herself so I can continue. "It's possible I was. I was trying to remember the state of my lips and breath. We'd both just had hot chocolate, so we would likely taste the same to each other, right? There had been no onions at dinner and no chewing gum at any point."

She unmutes and reappears on screen sans-cereal. "If Wade walked in right now and kissed you like the world was ending in a moment via the solar flare we all know is coming, would you care what he tasted like?"

"No?"

"Sand, no. You wouldn't. Trust me, Dr. Vampire knows how to kiss, and when he does, you won't care if there's a bit of coffee flavor in there, or mint or chocolate. As long as he's not a smoker. Is he a smoker?"

"No." We both shudder at the thought.

Avery appears behind Lee. "And what does your *teacher* say?"

My chest aches at the two of them there, together, without me.

Not for the first time, I wonder if in my rush to achieve and advance and just keep moving, maybe I made a misstep. What if I'd gone a little slower, made ninety-fives instead of one hundreds, would I be happier?

"Well?" Lee prods.

I shake off my mood. No point dwelling on what cannot be changed. "I haven't heard from him, actually. He didn't ask for a status report."

Lee nods. "Good. The more space you put between you and he, the better."

"I think it's *between you and him*," Avery corrects.

We discuss which one is correct for a few minutes, eventually deciding we are, in fact, the dorkiest of the dorks, having let a perfectly good discussion about boys and kissing devolve into a debate about grammar. We laugh. Lee snorts.

I miss them.

I miss Jonny, too.

I minimize my friends' faces and send him a text.

Me: Are you alive? It has been over twenty-four hours without an animated gif from you. Please respond before I am forced to notify the Tulsa Police Department.

"Sand? Herllro?" Lee is back into the cereal. "When is your next date?"

"Oh. I don't know. His schedule is overfull. I don't know how he manages it."

Avery waves a hand. "The man's gotta eat. He'll text you. But—and please don't bite my head off, either of you—can we revisit the makeover idea?"

Lee drops the spoon in her bowl with a clang. "Ave! She is fine the way she is!"

"I know she's fine! I'm talking about a haircut and few new tops, not a personality transplant!"

"Hey, I went with the shirt you sent. He loved it."

"Loved, you say?" Avery puts a hand to her ear. "Come again?"

"He looked at my cleavage multiple times and whispered in my ear that I couldn't wear the shirt to class."

My friends are so still on my screen I wonder if our connection has frozen.

"That's so hot," Avery finally whispers.

"Unbelievably so. I am having mean, jealous thoughts right now."

I laugh at Lee's serious expression and direct my thoughts to Avery. "But maybe new tops are not enough?"

She grimaces. "Welllll, it was quite an ordeal to get you to wear a low-cut, long-sleeve sweater with pants and boots and a parka. I just think you need to get bold! Get brave! Think about how much difference contacts made, Sand."

I adjust my glasses instinctually. "Lee. She has a point."

"Ugh, well, who is going to facilitate this magical transformation? Not us, even if we had the skills, which we don't—"

"Hey, I—" Avery starts.

"No, Ave, you don't. And even if you did have the skills you think you do, we're not there. We can't do it over FaceTime. So who? Not Sandra's mom. Do you have any stylish aunts? Any friends with sisters?"

I chew on my thumbnail and think. The only stylish person I have had recent contact with is Layla. Obviously I'd rather have my epidermis removed via dull scalpel than ask her for help. But the thought of her gives me an idea.

"I think I have someone."

"Who?"

Before I can answer, Jonny begins responding to my text. I quickly say goodbye to my friends so I can open up his messages.

Jonny: Call off the search dogs!

Jonny: I'm alive, though just barely after a day of golf with my dad and brother yesterday.

Jonny: Then church and brunch this morning, you know, the usual.

Jonny: So? Mission Report?

Me: Success.

Jonny: Doors opened for you? Even car doors? Did he pull your chair out?

Me: Yes, yes, and yes.

Jonny: Good. How about music, any deal breakers?

Me: All of his favorites were acceptable.

Jonny: Good!

The three dots appear and disappear a few times. This has happened with Wade a few times, before he said something sweet. Hesitation when texting is normal for me, and sometimes Lee or Avery, too, if they are about to send something they know I won't like.

It's very unusual for Jonny.

Jonny: And did the end of the night go the way you wanted it to?

I hesitate. This feels much more normal, him waiting on me to formulate a response. My stomach is tight. Again, a familiar sensation. The night didn't end the way I wanted. I wanted Wade to kiss me. He didn't. Do I tell Jonny that?

No. I can't talk to Jonny about kissing, or rather *not* kissing, Wade. Maybe if we were emailing. Probably not even then.

Me: The end of the date was acceptable.
Jonny: OK good.

Something feels odd about our conversation. It's not just the slow replies on his part. It's also the end. I don't think he's ever sent just two words at the end of a conversation since we started texting. There's usually a meme or gif or sometimes even a link to a song that fits our discussion. I consider messaging him again, but my phone buzzes.

Wade: Hey, gorgeous!
Wade: I had a blast with you last night. I can't do it again until Saturday. Does that work for you?
Me: Hey, handsome.
Me: Yes, Saturday sounds great!

Saturday is perfect, as it allows me plenty of time to talk to my soon-to-be friend and complete my transformation.

"Excuse me," I say clearly to NotLayla in the hall after our Monday class. It's a miracle my voice isn't shaky. All of my insecurities from middle school and high school have resurfaced at the idea of asking the class pretty girl for help. This conversation could be humiliating. I am used to mean girls, so I can bounce back if everything goes wrong, but I hope I don't have to.

Wade made eye contact with me eight times during his lecture. After class, he watched me walk all the way out of the room. It was intense in a very good way. Each instance of eye contact solidified my resolve.

"Huh?"

"Hi, I'm Sandra." I extend a hand. She takes it and shakes firmly, even though her face is contorted. *Please don't be a mean girl, please don't be a mean girl.*

"Jenn."

"Hi, Jenn. Can I walk with you?"

"Sure, but, uh, what's up? I hope you're not looking for any kind of help. Because honestly I've actually been working up the nerve to ask *you* to tutor *me*."

What luck!

"Really? Well, I happen to be in need of a favor. Maybe we can come to an arrangement."

She stops walking and turns to me. "Oh man, you would really be saving my ass, so anything you need. Tell me."

"It's...not a small favor."

She straightens in anticipation. "Okaayyyy?"

"I was wondering if you could help give me a makeover."

She blinks rapidly, like Lee does sometimes, as if her brain is receiving too many signals and can't compute them all. Her mouth falls open. I am unsure if these reactions are positive or negative.

Finally, she asks, "Are you being serious?" I nod.

The emotion on her face transforms from confusion into what I would describe as glee. "Yes! Holy crap, this is going to be the most fun I've had since that Lambda Chi party my junior year of undergrad! I mean, listen, you are gorgeous, and you don't need a makeover, okay? Obviously. The patriarchy can shove their unrealistic beauty standards up their asses and all that. But honey, when I am done with you, this whole campus better watch the hell out!"

"So you agree? I tutor you and you help me with...girly stuff?"

"But...if I get the tutoring and I get to be your stylist, what's in it for you?"

What's in it for me? Was I unclear? "Wait, what?"

She starts giggling. "Sandra. I just mean I'd *love* to do it! Yes! When can we start!"

I look around to make sure Wade is nowhere near us. I realize I should've checked for him before starting this entire conversation. Luckily, the coast is clear.

"I have a date on Saturday night."

"Well, damn then, give me your phone number. I'll text you tonight!"

CHAPTER 13

"Is that him? Is Mr. Saturday night texting you?" Jenn asks quietly. We are in an upscale boutique where, apparently, we need to whisper.

"No, just a friend." I put my phone in my back pocket and focus on the rack in front of me. I don't actually pick anything out. In fact, I could just go sit by the dressing room, because Jenn has said I don't even have veto power over her choices for me.

"That didn't look like you were reading a message from a friend." I am not sure what she means, but she motions toward the dressing rooms before I can ask. "Let's go try these and see what we're working with."

She hoists the giant pile of clothes onto the bench in the dressing room. She straightens and looks me in the eye with purpose. "Remember, I need to see each option. No skipping!"

The very first item is a tight, short, sparkly black dress with spaghetti straps. I hate it. Still, I exit the dressing room and walk to the mirror where Jenn is perched on a small stool.

"Cute! How do you feel in this?"

"Itchy and nauseous."

"Nauseous! Okay. Good to know. So, before you take this off, look at your legs. They're bangin', girl. You're so long. Long legs, long torso. All of you is lean and twiggy. You can make that work for you."

I can see what she means about my lankiness. I pull at the itchy little strap on my shoulder. "So I don't have to wear this?"

"Definitely not! We want you to find some pieces that are Peak Sandra. You at your absolute best. If you don't feel confident in this, you won't look hot in this. You'll look itchy and nauseated, as you said. So let's find some things that make you feel like a queen."

I cycle through a few more dresses that I don't like. Or, as Jenn keeps saying, dresses that aren't Peak Sandra. Jenn and I talk through the dressing room curtains. She is easy to talk to. She makes fun of herself that she's "a typical airhead hoping to become a—wait for it—plastic surgeon." She explains she fell and broke her nose and frontal bones as a little girl and was fascinated that her doctor could put her back together like a doll.

She also shares, to my surprise, that she had considered introducing herself to me a few times but was intimidated. Apparently everyone knows about my young age and "big brain." She said I always seemed so focused, she didn't want to bother me. I feel badly for automatically assuming the pretty girl would be a mean girl. I tell her to quit making fun of herself as I walk out of the dressing room for the twelfth time.

"Now *this* looks amazing. Please tell me you like this one."

I observe the short, flowy jumpsuit on my frame. It's long-sleeved with a high scoop neck in a tiny maroon floral pattern. It's not tight, but the shorts are very short. It's not a dress, and yet it's the most feminine thing I've ever worn.

"It's perfect."

"Yassssss! Okay, let's find a few more like this!"

We do. We also find a few more plain tees with deep V-necks. I purchase two new push-up bras. I'm feeling energized as we head toward the check-out counter.

"You're really not going to tell me who your date is with? I mean, who cares if I know him, right?" Jenn starts rambling to herself. I learned during dinner last night and our shopping ex-cursion tonight that this is something she does. "Unless it's a professor? Ew, all our professors are like fifty years old. Well, I mean there are hot fifty-year-olds, I guess, like actors and stuff, but all of our professors are total cringe. No. Gotta be a student. Which brings me back to why on earth you won't tell me?"

"It's just new," I say as I swipe my card. "Our school is like a small town. Everyone talks. I'm not sure this is worth talking about yet."

"Okay, I'm hearing you say that you don't trust me, and that's fine, because we've known each other for, like, ten seconds, but I will worm my way into your heart and soon you're gonna tell me your whole life story, Sandra, believe me."

She smiles a huge smile at me.

I believe her.

After I get home, I enjoy a few minutes of blissful silence be-fore remembering I turned my phone off. Between notifications from Avery, Lee, Jonny, and Wade, I couldn't focus on the task at hand with Jenn. I hold the button until the rectangle in my hand comes to life. A second later, a FaceTime call comes in.

"Jonny?"

His face is tense. "Where the hell have you been?"

"I was shopping."

"Very funny. Seriously, Sand, I was really starting to get worried!"

"I turned my phone off so I could focus on what I was doing, which was shopping."

Jonny does a double-take at his phone camera. "Wait, you're serious?"

"Yeah."

He stares at me without talking. It's unusual. I let myself stare back, taking in his perfect features and the eyes I sometimes see when I close my own.

"Still not used to the contacts," he mutters softly. I begin to smile, and he smiles, too, but looks away. He fiddles with something I can't see on screen. "What exactly were you shopping for that was so important you had to turn off your phone?"

"New clothes."

He gives me a glare. "Seriously. If you don't want to tell me, Sand, just say so."

"I am serious! I was shopping for date clothes. As you'll recall, I was not properly dressed for our practice dinner, and the effects of that realization have snowballed."

He grimaces at something I can't see. "Oh, uh, good. I guess. Hey, it's late, I have an early morning, and I'm sure you have to study. But just don't go AWOL on me without a text next time, okay?"

"Okay."

"Night, Sandy."

"Good night."

I scan through the texts I missed during the shopping spree. Wade sent a few things but didn't seem to mind that I didn't write him back for hours. I decide Wade's reaction is actually more appropriate than Jonny's.

Me: Guess what.

Wade: What?

Me: I made a new friend. From class. You will never guess who it is.

Wade: A male friend?

Me: You'll see tomorrow. I'll sit next to them.

Wade: Okay. I wish you could sit next to me during class.

Me: There are no seats by you. I suppose I could sit on the desk?

Wade: Damn it, Gorgeous! Now that will be all I can think about during class.

Wade: How am I going to get through my lecture?

Me: I'm sorry?

Wade: I'm not. See you tomorrow.

Me: See you.

Wade: And I can't wait until Saturday.

Me: ;)

"Okay, so you're going to have to trust me on this." Jenn is bubbling over with excitement as we walk together after class. But

I'm distracted. Wade only made eye contact with me once during his lecture. It disappointed me more than I was expecting.

My phone buzzes as Jenn and I walk out of the building into the fresh air.

> Wade: You're right, I would not have guessed Jennifer!
>
> **Me: She is unexpected.**
>
> Wade: I don't like that seat, though. I couldn't stare at you like I wanted, in case she thought I was looking at her.
>
> **Me: Oh.**
>
> Wade: It was probably good practice for me, though. A study in restraint. ;)
>
> **Me: ;)**

I grin happily to myself as I tuck my phone away. I realize Jenn is talking to me.

"I mean, she looks like she might ride a Harley. Wait, actually I think she does ride a motorcycle. Does she? Anyway, I meant she has a lot of tattoos. And her accent sounds like she may drink lemonades on a porch in front of a cornfield with your grandmama. But! She knows hair. *And* she could get you in on short notice."

I stop walking. "All of the things you just said are very concerning."

She laughs and puts a hand on my shoulder. "Holy crap, you are hilarious. New favorite person alert! It's you!" She gives my shoulder a pat. "We're not chopping length off or doing anything drastic. Don't worry! I won't let you down."

I suspect the concern is still apparent on my face.

"Sand! I'm telling you! You have beautiful warm brown hair. We're going to add some subtle gold highlights around your face, and that's it... Well, and wax your brows...and maybe above your lip... You should see your face right now. If your Laterus Recti pull any farther back, your eyeballs are going to fall right out of the front of your face!"

I close my eyelids at the mention of them and start to shake my head. This whole makeover plan has gotten too ambitious. *I am not cut out for this. I should speak up and say no. I should say absolutely no hot wax on or anywhere near my face!*

But my eyes flash open as I am being led away by hand. Jenn is assuring me she'll take care of me. She points to the highlights in her own hair. She is rambling. Everything is a bit of a blur.

The afternoon continues on this way. Jenn and Heather, who looks and speaks exactly as described, talk at me about how beautiful I am. I am unconvinced. Hours pass in a whirlwind of chemicals, trimmings, blow dryers, and reassuring words.

I acquiesce to the waxing. I agree to the use of hot rollers, which Jenn insists I need to buy to use at home. I even nod when Heather asks to do my makeup. I don't think I've said more than "uh huh" or "okay" for hours. Not all that uncommon for me, but alarming given the circumstances.

Jenn squeals. "You're going to thank me in about twenty seconds, sister!"

Heather steps back from me. "Alrighty, darlin', you ready?"

I nod, but my face is tight. Heather turns my chair so I can see myself.

I...

I...

I...

"Well?!" Jenn asks while jumping up and down. I am tempted to get up and jump as well.

My eyes fill with tears.

It's me, just...I'm...

I manage to find my vocal cords. "Thhhhhank you."

I start crying fully, prompting Jenn to hand me a tissue.

"Well, now, don't start that." Heather sniffs. "You're fixin' to ruin my masterpiece!"

Jenn's eyes are misty, and her voice is quiet now. "Did I tell you or did I tell you? Peak Sandra. A. Freaking. Knock. Out."

I look in the mirror again. I feel a little silly for getting so emotional about a bit of strategically applied bleach. And wax. And is that blush, I guess?

In this moment, though, twelve-year-old Sandy, who wished her mom could help her, who longed for sisters, who prayed at night for a few genuine female friends...that girl finally got what she wanted. I have Avery and Lee, and now Jenn. In the mirror, I see myself, in vibrant, saturated color. I think it's as if before I was looking at a reflection on cloudy glass. It was muddled and not quite right. Now it's clear.

And the image reflected back is me.

Fully me.

And after the shock wears off, the first thought in my mind is, *I can't wait to show Jonny.*

"So, will you tell me who your date is yet? Haven't I earned it?" Jenn asks as we walk out of the salon.

I grin. "Think of the most attractive male you've encountered so far in all of our first-year classes."

She stops walking and stares off into the distance.

"WADE?!" she yells.

My grin becomes a smile. "Oh, I am *so* jealous." She is still yelling as she unlocks the car for us. "I am going to need a minute here. Many minutes. I mean, you are totally my girl and all, but, like, I had already picked out our kids' names!"

I laugh as she rails on. "I wrote Dr. Jenn Anderson in my notebook! And I'm pretty sure the two skanks one row down from me both did the same thing! Wow. Wowowowowow. Okay, okay, getting over the jealousy blackout now...I mean, my new best friend is dating the Wade Anderson! Oh, I cannot wait for every single detail of every moment you have with him from now on. This is amazing."

She spouts off a lot of words on the way home, but my favorites are *new best friend.*

CHAPTER 14

Jonny: Just out here supporting bugs and turtles!

The unexpected text disrupts my Thursday night activities, which include watching hot roller tutorials and testing various lip stains Jenn bought because "they're neither sticky, smelly, nor tasty." They sounded ideal.

I look at the next text that comes through. It's a group photo in front of a banner that reads *Oklahoma Wildlife Preservation Benefit*. I start to smile until I see next to Jonny's dad, mother, uncle, and brother, tucked into his arm like she belongs there, is Layla.

She looks stunning in a long blue dress that I don't think is formal enough to be called a gown. Whatever the classification, it's beautiful. Her blue eyes stand out almost as much as Jonny's, which appear bluish due to their proximity to her dress. His navy suit fits him as it should, since I'm sure it was tailored for his body by Juan, his favorite "suit guy."

Her beauty complements his so perfectly, I get lost in time, just staring the two of them. Until I realize my left thumb is burning on the edge of the roller in my hand. I curse and send a quick thumbs-up reaction to Jonny's image before dropping my phone down onto my bathroom counter.

I let out a groan of frustration as I run my thumb under cold water. Seeing them together should not still affect me so, not after so many years.

I have spent years examining these emotions. There was jealousy; that feeling was obvious. There was longing, to be seen by him the way Layla was, to be held. To be wanted in a way that disrupted the body's deep internal systems.

But in addition, there was rage. Dismay. Disbelief. Layla held the affections of Jonny Canton in her hands, and she'd tossed it aside to have sex with some baseball player at a fraternity party. It was incomprehensible. She was planet earth's prized idiot. The dumbest girl alive.

Though Jonny never did seem to be attracted to the smart ones, did he?

I glance up at myself in the mirror. Half of my head is covered in poorly secured rollers. My top lip is a different color than my bottom lip. The sides of my eyes are smudged with black after four failed attempts at a YouTuber's famous "Easy Sultry Cat-Eye Liner Technique."

Who am I even looking at? What the hell am I doing? I should be studying! I should be focused on my goals, my future! Mom was right. Vanity is a distraction rarely worth the time and attention it steals. She said that whenever I lingered too long in the lipstick aisle drugstore or picked up a fashion magazine in a waiting room.

I yank the curlers out of my hair and scoop my locks into a twist on the top of my head. In one quick motion of my forearm,

I slide all of the products strewn across the counter into a canvas bin. The efficiency pleases me. I shove the bin under my sink and slam off the bathroom light on my way out the door.

With a deep, focused breath, I sit at my coffee table and open my textbook to where I'd left the latest sticky tab. I study.

I study for days. I respond to text messages using the least amount of effort possible. Even Wade and Jonny only get emoji reactions.

On Saturday afternoon, Avery, Lee, and Jenn bombard me with messages. I don't reply. It's just a date. I have an exam on Tuesday that is much more important than getting Wade to kiss me. I remind myself of the exam over and over as the hours pass by.

But at five o'clock, when I open my door and find Jenn standing on my "Welcome, Hope You Like Books" door mat, curling iron and makeup bag in hand, I am relieved. And happy. And a bit annoyed at myself about those feelings.

"This is what happens when you ignore your best friend's texts," she walks in without my invitation. I can't help but smile. My smile fades when I remembered Jonny's similar words. *Why are thoughts of him always in my brain? C'mon, synapses! Do better!*

"You're wearing the dark red romper, right?" Jenn calls back to me as she heads to my bathroom.

"I had planned on jeans. It's still pretty cold out."

Jenn's head pops out of the bathroom. "Peak Sandra is not concerned with a little chill. The car is warm, the restaurant is warm, wear a coat, and if you get cold, cozy up to the world's hottest TA, for shit's sake!"

"Peak Sandra sounds reckless," I deadpan back to her.

She ignores me and disappears back into the bathroom. I glance into the little room from the hall and watch her begin organizing cosmetics next to my sink. Her curling iron is already plugged in and heating. I cock my head at it.

Jenn is triumphant. "I knew you wouldn't actually use the rollers."

I agree to relinquish control of my hair to her but insist on minimal makeup. She agrees, but I feel my plan misfire when she smirks and insists I do the applying myself. This is what I get up for speaking up. She is patient and helpful, and together we pull achieve almost the same result with Heather earlier in the week. I am almost as pleased as Jenn is with our handiwork.

"Sand." She turns back to me in seriousness as she walks out my door an hour later. "This is for all womankind everywhere. You gotta bag this guy. Get Wade off the market so we're all taken out of our misery, okay?"

I just roll my eyes at her. I have some time before Wade arrives, so I straighten up my apartment. It's not messy, but there are a few dishes sitting out, books laying open, etcetera. When everything is tidy, I feel better. I respond to everyone's messages that I ignored during the day, except Jonny's.

Jonny: This thing was an hour from my meeting. I don't know if I love it or hate it.
Jonny: [Photo of praying mantis sculpture in Pennsylvania]
Sandra Loved an Image
Jonny: Are you sure you don't want to use your big brain to figure out teleportation for me?

Jonny: [Photo of a long line at the airport]

Sandra disliked an image

Jonny: Do you have a big test coming up?

Jonny: ...or maybe a big date coming up?

Jonny: How do I know someone hasn't stolen your phone and is only reacting to my messages so I'll think you're still alive?

Me: Quit watching true crime specials.

Jonny: Prove you're really Sandra Hayes.

I don't send him a selfie. For some reason, I just can't bring myself to really engage with him. Not since the benefit photo.

A knock at the door is a welcome redirection of my attention. I glance at myself quickly in a small decorative mirror on the wall. I'm pleased to find that lip stain does look like lipstick, without any residue. It's as if Jenn just put it on, even though I drank some water after she left.

Peak Sandra. I open my door.

Wade is as handsome as ever in a black jacket, black shirt, and dark jeans. *Smart, sexy vampire, indeed.* When my eyes finally reach his face, I'm taken aback. Wade looks almost distraught. His eyes are wide first, then hooded.

"Whoa," he whispers. His big brown irises go down my face all the way to the short boots, back up my exposed legs, over the romper, and back to my face.

His hands drop to his sides, one of which is holding a small box of chocolates. It's a strange motion, as if his brain could no longer concentrate on supporting the weight of his hands. I can't hold back my smile. He reaches out a hand to touch me but freezes with it hanging between us, unsure. "You changed your hair?"

"Jenn." I raise one shoulder. The connection between my appearance and my new friendship should be obvious. He moves his suspended hand to his face where he rubs a finger along his full lips.

"Well, I'm going to have to flunk her now, obviously." He is still talking softly. His hands move back to the chocolate box. He takes a step toward me.

I feel my internal organs trying to sink down into my legs. "You don't like it?" I look down and shuffle backward a bit.

A warm, large hand finds my cheek. Wade's voice is smooth and soft. "What will I call you now? Gorgeous will no longer suffice." My smile returns slowly. I notice he's moved closer to me. Much closer. The edges of my breasts are touching his chest. His eyes search mine, and as my smile appears, so does his. I feel my pulse thrashing in my ears.

Wade clears his throat and moves back two inches. "Truffles, but none with fruit flavors. Harder to find than you might think."

"Thank you." I take the chocolates and enjoy the touch of our hands as I do so. I put them on the counter and grab my coat from the hook by the door.

"Shall we?" he asks.

We make our way through the hall, into the elevator, and out of the entrance with Wade's eyes on me almost the entire time. I expected him to trip, as his eyes were never on the ground in front of him. He was staring without reservation or embarrassment. I think his intensity would be unsettling to most people. I don't mind it.

He opens the passenger door of his car for me but stops me with his arm before I can climb in.

He inhales, with effort. "You're sensational, Sandra… All of my senses are affected." His voice is buttery and lovely.

"You affect me, too," I reply softly. I cheer internally that I get the words out without issue. I also make a mental note to thank Jenn for everything, including her insistence on scented lotion.

We have a lovely dinner together. Wade is just as animated as I am when he talks about our studies and crazy medical stories he's heard of or read about. But there are also long stretches of silence throughout the evening, and neither of us minds.

Wade suggests coffee, and I agree. I notice women eyeing him as we leave the restaurant and again when we enter the corner cafe. He is a beautiful man. Meticulous, too. His fingernails are clean and trimmed. He eats and drinks slowly, never needing the napkin he keeps folded on his knee. He keeps a small money clip instead of a wallet. Even his shoes are without a scuff. It surprises me when at one point in the night I have the urge to step on his foot, just to see a spot of imperfection on him somewhere. I refrain.

After coffee, he takes me home, offering to walk me all the way to my door. When I reach it, before fumbling for my keys, I gather my courage and turn to face him. *This is it!* I am excited and nervous and hopeful. I want Wade to kiss me. I want to be kissed. I want to be wanted by this tall, beautiful genius.

His eyes meet mine, then drop to my lips. He licks his lips before talking softly. "Thanks for a great night, Gorgeous." He smiles a small, mischievous grin. "Sorry. My brain has already cemented the pathways between you and that nickname."

"I like it." I am looking at his lips. I actually can't look away from his lips. I want to be ready! I see his smile widen and then fade as he takes a step closer. I barely feel his hands as he puts his fingers on either side of my face. They're spread out, as if he's holding my head up for me. My knees are a bit weak, so perhaps he is. His touch is feather light, however, so I'm not sure his hold is adequate for that task.

I keep watching his mouth as it moves closer. Then I can't watch anymore as my eyelids close and his velvety lips are on mine. They're cold but not sticky or wet. He presses his mouth on mine, one, two, three times. I tense, waiting for his tongue to push my lips open, but he pulls back.

"Sensational," he whispers, and then he flashes me his devastating set of perfect white teeth. I smile, too, pushing away my confusion. "I can't wait a whole week this time. Can I see you tomorrow?"

I nod.

He places a firm kiss on my forehead, then one on each cheek, and removes his hands.

"Good night, Sandra."

"Good night."

He backs away but keeps watching me. Again, I am concerned he will stumble. He motions with his eyes to my door. I fish out my keys, and when the door is open, I wave to him. He waves back and then turns around to go to the elevator.

I send Lee, Avery, and Jenn the same three words.

Me: Mission Report: SUCCESS!

I can't bring myself to send Jonny anything. I am unsure if this is a sign of a progression or regression. Soon the answer becomes obvious.

CHAPTER 15

I woke up Sunday morning wondering why Wade hadn't really kissed me at the conclusion of our date. I observed all the signs that he was attracted to me. He complimented my appearance multiple times throughout the night. At times his stare ventured into the classification of gawking. Yet with his kiss good night, there was no tongue, no groping, no passion.

Enough of this, Brain!

I showered. I read. I worked on my memorization for anatomy. I even, in a bout of homesickness, listened to a sermon. It was Sunday, after all. Which just made me think of brunch and Jonny in a suit jacket and, inevitably, Layla.

Layla next to him on the church pew. Layla in the passenger seat of his truck. Layla beside him at brunch. Layla getting kissed at the end of a date *with tongue*. There wouldn't be any holding back. If Jonny wanted something, reason abandoned him. When he was very young, he told me once, his compulsion had led him to shoplifting bubblegum. Jon Senior made Jonny return the gum, apologize, and intern at the shop for a week without pay. He simply took action. He probably kissed her until she couldn't breathe. He probably...

I said enough!

The subsequent buzz of my phone makes me feel as though Jonny sensed my thoughts. Illogical, of course. My thoughts often are, when it comes to him.

> Jonny: So what last night date number two???
> **Me: Yes.**
> Jonny: No status report? That bad?
> **Me: It was good.**

The three dots appear and disappear twice before Jonny finally responds.

> Jonny: Good, but I think as payment for your tutelage you should start attending brunch again. Robot Rob has already insulted Grandpa, pissed off the waiter, and reorganized the silverware around his plate. And no one is laughing silently with their eyes with me!
> **Me: Did you disrupt his forks when he wasn't looking?**
> Jonny: Absolutely I did, and you're missing it!

It takes all of my willpower to keep from asking him why Layla isn't laughing with him about it. Does she not notice or not find it funny? Is she not there? If not, why not?

I have to get myself out of these cyclical thoughts. Perhaps Lee was right and it was better when my friendship with Jonny had been reduced to short weekly emails. But that was when sixteen hundred miles separated us. And I'd missed him so deeply I felt a physical response in my body, like a chemical imbalance. Still, perhaps that was preferable to this renewed heartbreak.

> **Me: That is unfortunate, but I really do have to study.**
> Jonny: On Sundays?
> **Me: Every day.**
> Jonny: [Animated GIF Hello My Name is Lame]
> **Me: Nice chatting to you, Lame, but I have to go.**

I put my phone into do not disturb mode before he can pull me back in with his conversation pixels. As I've practiced so many times before, I clear my mind of all thoughts other than observations of my body and its surroundings. Once my breathing is deep and uniform, I open my textbook and begin.

Hours pass quickly before a knock sounds on my door. Wade waits on my doorstep in a thin athletic shirt, pants designed for running, and bright Nike sneakers. He could have stepped out of an advertisement for any one of the items he's wearing. Something in my brain registers how his lean muscles shift and ripple under the shirt as he lifts a bag of to-go food up with a shrug.

"Study break?" His smile is wide but tentative. "I tried to text and call, but I assumed you were in the zone."

"I was." I step back to let him in.

"And did you forget to eat? Or is that bad habit mine alone?"

My eyebrows jump into my hairline. "Not yours alone. I'm actually starving."

"I wasn't sure what you'd want, so I got a few options," he explains. I watch Wade unpack the Styrofoam boxes onto the bar, noting how similar his organizational decisions are to my own. He lines the containers up from largest to smallest, with all the straight lines perfectly parallel. Finally he takes out a stack of napkins—that he likely won't need—and places them at the end of his neat line.

I get us glasses of ice water, and we eat in mostly silence. Wade finishes his burger before I finish my chicken. He walks around the bar and asks me which subject I was reviewing as he washes his hand at his sink. While I finish my meal, he quizzes me. He shoots questions at me quickly, modulating the degree of difficulty. He tries to stump me. He doesn't. It's thrilling for us both.

We move to the couch and study together, me in my books and Wade on his phone. We sit close together, our thighs touching. He looks up from his phone occasionally to brush my hair from my face or stroke his hand down my back. He refills our waters. He forces us to take a break and walk the sidewalks surrounding my apartment for fifteen minutes. In the middle of our walk, he stops and pulls me into him with urgency.

Finally, Wade kisses me with his tongue. Everything about the kiss is controlled, measured, and careful, except for the moan in his throat. It breaks on its way out of his vocal cords. It sounds almost painful.

I assume he is holding back from kissing me the way he really wants to. I hear a car drive by and wonder if this is odd, to be kissing out in the street. Then I tense, realizing any passersby on foot or in vehicles could be a fellow student or faculty member.

Wade pulls back with his brow twisted tight. "Gorgeous?"

"We're outside." I look around us quickly but don't see any cars or people near us.

"Astute observation, Doctor."

I smile, but I remain tense. I don't know what the rules are regarding fraternization between teaching assistants and students. I do vividly remember, however, a girl in undergrad who was criticized without mercy for her relationship with a young professor. All manners of impropriety were implied, especially where the merit of her grades were concerned.

Wade recognizes my unease and resumes our walk. We study until it's time for another meal and another walk. I watch him on our stroll, and he keeps his distance with a smirk.

As soon as I close the door to my apartment upon our return, he kisses me. I guess he has been fighting the urge to do so all evening, yet still, he is controlled. His tongue sweeps mine three times, then he adjusts the alignment of our faces, then three strokes again. I lean into the predictability of it, moving with him. My body heat spikes, and Wade moans again before letting me go.

We study until late into the night. My eyes start to close, and the words on the page blur. This happens often, so I don't think much of it. Falling asleep on my books is perhaps more regular for me than falling asleep in my actual bed. Wade nudges me and says he should go home and I should go to sleep. He kisses me again at the door. One two three, adjust, one two three, adjust. It's warm and pleasant, and I grow so heavy it's as if he's kissing me to sleep. With a small chuckle, he kisses my forehead, then each cheek, and leaves.

I grab my phone on my way to quickly brush my teeth before collapsing from exhaustion. I can see I missed a few messages, but I only actually read the most recent one that is displayed.

Jonny: Study break? You never sent a selfie confirming proof of life yesterday. Guess I gotta come check your pulse myself.

I drop my toothbrush. I re-read the message, and my hand goes to my carotid arteries. Has Jonny ever touched my neck? Would he actually put his thumb there? My body heat spikes again, but this time it remains high.

So high that I can't fall asleep, despite being unable to keep my eyes open only moments ago. I clear my mind of all thoughts and focus on my breathing. That isn't enough. I adjust the thermostat in my apartment and turn on the fan. Sleep finally overtakes my consciousness.

When I wake up, my hand is resting lightly on my throat.

CHAPTER 16

Two weeks pass by in a stressful blur. I go to class, the library, Jenn's apartment, and home. When I'm at my apartment, so is Wade. We have formed a rhythm of eating, walking, and studying together. He kisses me often now. A couple times he's accosted me on the couch, mumbling that he couldn't help himself. He's pushed me onto my back and even caressed my chest and backside on top of my clothes. He's gentle but precise. *Swipe, swipe, swipe, adjust. Stroke, stroke, stroke, squeeze. Kiss, kiss, kiss, moan.*

Lee and Avery have been in a haze of test prep themselves, checking in only to ask very specific questions about Wade. I indulge them. They need the small bursts of endorphins to get them through the long days, like my texts from Jonny.

He's been traveling, which always leads to the most preposterous selfies and random photos. He claims he only sends what reminds him of me, and when he's traveling it seems that includes almost anything and everything.

He has also inquired about Mission Boyfriend, as he's calling it now. He never uses Wade's proper name. I give him as little information as possible, for reasons I can't exactly pinpoint. I have an instinct to keep Wade and Jonny separate.

Which is why Jonny's incoming message causes a violent fight-or-flight response in me. I get up and walk around, subconsciously choosing flight.

> Jonny: I told Layla about our mission, and she wants to go on a double date. It's probably time I observe my student out in the wild, don't you think?

I don't respond. Hours later, he messages again.

> Jonny: C'mon, Sand, I want to meet this guy.
> **Me: When? We have exams.**
> Jonny: After your next big test, then.
> **Me: Let me ask him.**

I almost couldn't believe my own fingers. As an introvert with clear goals requiring extreme dedication, I learned a valuable lesson early in life: "no" is a complete sentence. Why didn't I just use it? Why does Jonny somehow always get what he wants? Especially from me?

> **Me: Would you be open to a double date with my friend Jonny and his gf next weekend?**
> Wade: Jonny, the childhood best friend? Sure.

I recoil at Wade's label for the biggest, brightest person in my life. I don't respond that Jonny is still my best friend in adulthood and would be until I am an octogenarian. Or beyond, if I live that long. Perhaps medical nanobots will become viable in my mid-life. It's a thrilling new field of study that is almost as interesting to me as orthopedics...

Focus, Sandra!

I set up a date and time with both Wade and Jonny, letting the latter pick the place. He chooses a nice restaurant on the far north side of the city. I close the text conversations. Thoughts of this impending explosion, the collision of separate worlds, will have to wait until after my two tests.

I am able to clear my thoughts. Almost.

I smooth the new dress down over my bony hips. After a passionate group text, it was decided I needed something new. This black wrap dress is soft and flowing like the rompers I love but feels a bit more dressy. It is low cut enough to be alluring but not revealing and short enough to "show off," as Jenn said. She—now a style mentor to not just myself but Avery and Lee as well—convinced me it was warm enough to trade my heavy coat for her stylish denim jacket. I won the small battle over foot-wear, convincing my three friends that I was not ready for any kind of heel beyond my favorite short suede boots.

Tonight is about finding and maintaining my Peak Sandra confidence. Not for Wade or Jonny but for myself, even when sit-ting across the table from Layla. Even if I have to endure watch-ing Jonny stare at her like she hung the moon...listen to her ev-ery word...touch her when she dared call herself his girlfriend but then touched another. He may have forgiven her, but I am unsure I ever will.

Wade arrives exactly at six thirty and upon seeing me pulls me in for three long, hard, tongue-less kisses. He pulls away and gazes up and down my body in vampire-like fashion. It still makes me light-headed, to be wanted in this way. I wonder if tonight is the night he'll finally venture his perfect fingers under my clothes.

When we pull up to the restaurant, my cardiovascular system absorbs all of my nerves, pumping furiously and sporadically. It is enough for me to make an appointment about a possible arrhythmia. I also begin to sweat profusely. As I remove the denim jacket, Wade asks for a refresher on our party for the evening.

"His name is Jonny and what's her name again?"

"Lllll..."

"Gorgeous? Hey, why are you nervous?" Wade grabs my hand in his and looks at me with warm concern. "Did you and Jonny ever..."

"No." I take a few deep breaths.

"So is this about the girlfriend, then?"

I nod. "We went to high school togethhhher. She was..."

"A bitch?"

I wince. She honestly was a bit of a bitch. She wasn't as overtly mean to me as some of the other girls on the cheer squad with her, but I knew that was only because of my close friendship with the star quarterback. It's hard to describe the girl who is *that* girl. The pretty, intimidating girl in school. The flirty, bubbly girl everybody admired from afar. I think through the catalog of images from high school.

"They were homecoming king and queen, and I was, well..."

"Already graduated and thriving at Stanford?" He squeezes my hand.

I smile wide, and the first calming breath fills my lungs. I take another deep breath, and another.

"Sandra, I know he's a good friend, but we can cancel. I can meet him some other time."

"No, it's all right." I squeeze his hand. "Layla. Her name is Layla. Let's go."

Wade opens the door for me and pulls me up into his arms. He kisses my forehead, nose and mouth. One, two, three. He takes my jacket out of my nervous grip and folds it neatly over one arm before leading me through the parking lot with my fingers in his. When we get to the door, he lets go of my hand and moves his to my lower back. I feel fortified. Safe. Then I see them.

Jonny and Layla stand at the hostess stand, having just walked in themselves. It's a Friday night, so the hostess is talking with him about finding us a table. Layla looks up and immediately notices Wade. Her eyes go over his whole body quickly, then back up to his face, where her gaze lingers too long. She smiles a coy, small grin before looking down at me. She studies me for three whole seconds without a hint of recognition.

"Holy shit, *Sandra*?!"

I manage to say hey in response to her awkward outburst. Wade's hand moves from my back to my waist. He squeezes tightly, but I hardly feel it. I can't help but watch Jonny as he turns, confused. He looks past me for a second before he looks at me. His confusion deepens and then turns to surprise? Shock?

His eyes look me over quickly. It's not a sensual perusal like the one Layla just gave my date. It looks more like he doesn't trust the relay of images from his eyes to his mind. His mouth falls open, and he rears his torso back as if he's been hit.

"Wow, what happened to you? Like, you look *amazing*! Did you go on, like, a makeover show or like get a stylist or something?"

Wade squeezes me again before clearing his throat and letting go of me. He extends his hand. "You must be Layla."

"Yes! Hi! Yes, sorry, it's just we've known each other since we were like twelve and I just never, uh, um..."

"I understand the effect. She's a beautiful woman. I'm Wade."

At the sound of Wade's name, Jonny's internal systems seem to have finished resetting. Through the entire exchange, he just stared at me. I had to smile and look away at the intensity of it, of him. I look back now as he assesses my date.

"*You're* the boyfriend?" Layla shrieks the question.

Wade smiles back at me. "I suppose I am, yes." He turns and extends his hand to Jonny.

"Hey, man, Jon Canton. Nice to meet you." Jonny's voice sounds garbled, but he's started to turn on his usual charm.

Wade steps to the side so I can step up and join them at the hostess counter. "Likewise, Sandra has told me all about you."

I have? I haven't. That's an odd thing for Wade to lie about.

"She has, huh? ...Sandra." Jonny utters my name in a way he never has before in the nearly fourteen years I've known him. It sounds like he asked my name as a question but also claimed it like a declaration. The sound of it, and their combined stares, has the skin of my face burning many degrees hotter than the rest of my body.

"Hey, g-guys." I look between the three of them until Layla reaches in to hug me as if we're friends. I move from her to hugging Jonny hello, like I have a thousand times before. He freezes. He doesn't hug me back at all. I step back awkwardly, and Wade steps up behind me with the support of his hand. I feel an itchy discomfort at how close we're all standing.

"Uhhhh, your table's ready." The hostess breaks the tension.

Jonny is closest to her, then myself and Wade and then Layla, who stepped back so Jonny and I could hug. Jonny turns from the waitress to me.

"Please, ladies first."

I almost jump ahead to escape the pressure building in the tiny vestibule. After I take a few steps, Jonny turns to follow me in front of Layla and Wade.

"Pff, Jon!" Layla lightly hits Jonny's chest as Wade clears his throat.

"Sorry, babe," Jonny grunts absently. I hear Layla's heels clack behind me as I follow the hostess to our cozy booth in the back of the restaurant. Layla slides in, and I hesitate. Sitting on the inside of the booth as a left-handed person is irritating to both booth occupants.

"Let me." Wade smiles, sliding in so I can sit on the outside.

"Oh, that's right, you're a lefty! I always forget. Is that, like a weird genius thing or is it just a you thing?" Layla asks.

"Layla," Jonny scolds.

"Sandra is the exception in almost every way, isn't she? Left-handedness suits her, I think." Wade squeezes my thigh with his hand under the table. Layla makes a strange sound that fills the beat of terribly tense silence.

"So." Jonny takes his seat. "Uh, you're in class with Sandy? You're not a freshman."

"Technically, I am in class with her." Wade smirks at me, as if this entire evening is an inside joke between him and me. Jonny glares at him with intense distaste.

I can't help but let out a nervous laugh. "He's the TA. Wade is a fourth year."

For some reason, this displeases Jonny even more. "Wait, so you're, what, twenty-six?"

Wade holds steady, heated eye contact with Jonny. "Twenty-four."

"Oh, you're twenty-four, Jon's twenty-three, I'm twenty-two, and soon Sandy will be twenty-one! Cute!"

Wade and Jonny continue their stare-down.

"He graduated early, too," I blurt, hoping it will help. It doesn't.

"Huh." Jonny finally breaks eye contact. "Just never thought Sandy's first boyfriend would be an older guy."

"I am just shocked *you're* her first boyfriend!" Layla chimes in with an obnoxious giggle.

Wade turns to me with a small smile. "I'm shocked by that as well." He moves his hand from my thigh to put it around my shoulders, pulling me into him as kisses me on the side of my head, then squeezes my shoulder twice. Jonny stares at the motion with an unreadable expression.

The server comes by to get our drink orders. Jonny gets a beer, Layla gets a fruity cocktail, and Wade and I get waters.

"Oh, man," Layla gushes after the server confirms two waters. "You two are just perfect for each other. Aren't they, Jonny? I'm just loving this for you, Sand."

"Uh huh." Jonny grunts.

"Seriously, though, who did your makeover? I need names and numbers."

I stammer for a second, noticing the differences between us. Layla's blond hair is long and stick-straight. It's so shiny the small table light reflects in it like a mirror. My light, golden-brown hair flows past my shoulders in barely tamed natural waves that Jenn heartily approved of via text. They seem frizzy to me now. And while Layla's face looks airbrushed under expertly applied makeup and what I'm fairly certain are false eyelashes, I have on blush, mascara, an eyeshadow stick, and lip stain. I couldn't figure out how to put on foundation to cover my freckles without looking orange, so I skipped it.

"And, like, this is the first time I've ever seen you in a dress, I think. Ever!" Layla is interrupted by the arrival of our drinks. While the server places the drinks, Wade leans in and breathes into my ear.

"How's it feel to be the smartest *and* the prettiest girl in the room by far? Because it feels pretty damn good to be your date." He gives me three quick kisses under my ear before pulling away to peruse the menu.

Goose bumps erupt all over my entire body down to the tops of my toes. I'm just not sure if Wade's hot words evoked them or the look on Jonny's face as he watches my boyfriend.

I've seen that emotion on that perfect face before, hot and murderous.

It's jealousy.

CHAPTER 17

When the appetizer arrives, some of the tension has dissipated. I am hopeful about the rest of the evening. As much as his momentary flare of jealousy messed with my lung capacity, Layla is still plastered onto his side like a tacky tattoo. I need to get this night over with and go back to the separation between my life and my friendship with Jonny.

We dig into the chips. Wade's hand is loose on my thigh, and Jonny's expression has relaxed, if only slightly. Layla interrogates my date about med school and Wade's upcoming internship or residency. Jonny listens, but whenever I steal a quick glance at him, he is looking at me, not Wade or his date.

"And you, Jonny? Canton as in Canton Cards, right?" Wade takes a big bite of artichoke dip, as if needing a reprieve from talking. Jonny takes a bite at the same time, so he only nods.

"It's Jon," I correct. Jonny's eyes flash to mine. I wonder if it feels as weird for him to hear it as it feels for me to say it. "His dad started the company because his mom, Jonny's, uh, Jon's grandma, she loved cards and letters. She'd write witty little notes for her boys. Jon's uncle helps, too, and his brother." Wade nods at me, so I continue. "Jon will be CEO eventually."

"Um, what?" Layla laughs. "Rob is already a vice president. Everyone knows Rob is going to take over. Jon isn't good with all the numbers and strategy. He's just good at sales. Right, babe?"

"Right," Jonny says, looking up and out as if searching for our server.

"Rob's the smart one, but Jonny's the hot one." She giggles again, running a hand up Jonny's chest.

I scoff. "More than numbers and strategy, businesses are built with people. Employees, buyers, franchisees, *customers*. Rob hates people. And people hate Rrrob. And Jonny, sorry, Jon, is every bit as smart as he is, too. And Rob knows it. That's why he's such a d-d-dick."

This topic has always made me angry. This might be the second time I've ever said the word dick. Wade's surprise is apparent on his face. That and some other emotion I can't quite pinpoint. But everyone in Jonny's life speaks about him and his brother this way, including his idiot girlfriend. And they're all wrong.

"Well, shit. Okay, then." Layla slurps up the last of her drink. Wade stares down at me, then looks at Jonny.

All the hardness in Jonny's expression melts for a moment. His voice is scratchy and quiet under the sounds of Layla's straw. "You can still call me Jonny."

Wade takes a sip of water and sets down his glass with a thud. "How did you two meet again?"

Jonny's face lights up. He loves to tell how I was "just out in the street, begging to die," as if I was flipping off a tornado in my front yard. He turns into Fun Jonny at the table, telling Wade story after story about us from our childhood. Layla chimes in with a couple stories of her own, but no one can hold a table's attention like Jonny can. She grows bored and makes a show of sucking down two more cocktails.

Wade listens and chuckles along, not laughing like Jonny and I do, but appreciative of the stories. He watches me and my reactions, along with Jonny's and Layla's. By the time dessert comes, which Jonny insists we all get, I get the sensation that Wade is sitting outside of a scene, observing.

Just as I'm about to pivot the conversation with questions for Wade, the server comes by with the receipt for dinner.

Wade stiffens. "Where's our half of the bill?"

"Oh, my dad plays golf with the owner. Don't worry about it."

Still statuesque, Wade turns to me. "In that case, are you ready to go, Gorgeous?"

"Sure." I smile up at him. He looks angry in a way that is incredibly attractive. I try to focus on his eyes and not the teal pair sending daggers at us from across the table. They are angry, too.

I get out of the booth to stand, and Jonny stands, too, leaning toward me slightly. "You guys don't want to get coffee or something?"

Wade puts his hand around my waist before saying, "I'm not sure Layla is up for coffee."

We all turn to look. Layla hiccups. "Wha?"

Wade turns and grabs my jacket from the booth and puts it over my shoulders before extending a hand to Jonny. "Thanks for dinner, Jon. We'll get the next one."

"Yeah, thanks," I add.

Jonny looks a bit panicked as he turns from Layla back to us to shake Wade's hand.

"Um, yeah, okay, well, bye, Sandy." Jonny starts to move in to hug me but stops as Wade tucks me into his side and turns us toward the exit.

"Bye. Bye, Layla," I say as I turn.

The drive back across town is awkward, tense, and silent. When we get close to my apartment, Wade sighs. I can't decipher what the sigh means.

Finally, he speaks. "That was...interesting." I let out an awkward laugh, unsure of what to say. When he gets to the doors of my apartment complex, he stops and looks at me. "So, Gorgeous, am I?"

I have no idea what he means.

"I'll see you tomorrow, *Girlfriend?*" He smirks, but his eyes and voice are serious. The moment he asks the question, I think of the girl from undergrad whose reputation was ruined in a matter of days. She disappeared from our class and didn't come back for the remainder of that semester. The professor, conversely, seemed completely unaffected.

He isn't angry about my hesitation. He hugs me and cradles my head on his chest. He kisses the top of my head once and my ear twice and whispers, "Good night, Gorgeous." He releases me and goes back to his car. He doesn't look back.

I head inside, confused. I make my way into my apartment, shrug out of my bra, put on a tank and sweats, and brush my teeth. I'm staring at my reflection, wondering if the entire night was one big mistake, when my phone buzzes.

Jonny: First double date! What'd you think??

Me: Well, you let your date get intoxicated, and I clearly did something wrong as well.

Jonny: What do you mean you did something wrong? What did he say?

I don't want to tell Jonny that Wade didn't kiss me good night. Also, I do want to tell him.

I want to tell him that he has only kissed me with his tongue a few times and I'm not sure if I kiss back like I'm supposed to, since Wade never loses his composure. I want to tell him that there's something keeping Wade—my boyfriend?—from trying to get to the sexual milestone I understand is called second base. I want to ask Jonny what exactly is wrong with me.

But the thought of sharing any of that is terrifying. So I put my phone into do not disturb mode and focus on some homemade flash cards to clear my mind of all the mental clutter... Jonny's face when he saw me in the lobby. His burning eyes when Wade kissed my neck. And when I called him Jon. The softness in his voice when he said I could still call him Jonny. The way he—

Wade knocks on my door. I check my reflection, and it's decent. My hair is up and falling out of the bun around my face, but it looks intentional. My makeup is still intact, even the lip stain. I debate putting on a bra but decide against it. My small mounds look good in the ribbed fabric of the tank top.

I open the door.

Jonny?

"Are you all right?" he pants, leaning against the door frame with one on each side of the opening. The jacket he wore at dinner is gone, leaving him in a tight black shirt and jeans. His muscles bulge out from under the fabric like they long to escape.

I nod, confused. "W-Where's Layla?"

"I dropped her at our hotel room." He pushes off the door and comes in. When I shut the door and turn around to face him, he notices my PJs for the first time. Under his stare, I feel my skin pull tight, including underneath my very thin top. His eyes rest on my nipples for a second before closing and then opening to look me square in the face.

Teal. Dark and swirling and I can't look away. He looks very... bothered, and I'm still not sure why. "What are you d-d-d-doing here?"

"I've told you, you can't just DND me, Sand. I was worried he said something, did something to you, I don't know! I wasn't sure, so I just came over as fast as I could."

"Oh."

"Yeah, oh! Now tell me what the hell you meant when you said you did something wrong before I lose my mind over here!"

I am able to break eye contact now. "Um, it, I... You didn't need to—"

"Sandy! Tell me!" he yells.

"He didn't kiss me good night! That's all! It wasn't a big deal!" The silence seems tangible after my outburst. No one has ever made me actually yell in exasperation except for Jonny. Not even when my parents irked me as a teenager. I stare at my feet while Jonny stares at me. He takes a small step forward.

"He didn't?" he asks softly.

I shake my head.

He takes two steps toward me, and I feel his heat down the front of my body. Jonny has always run hot like a furnace. Physically and emotionally.

Jonny swallows audibly. He reaches out his hands slowly. "He didn't say, 'I had a good time tonight.'" It's a whisper as I try to shake my head. I can't think clearly because he lightly runs his fingers from my wrists all the way up to my shoulders.

He moves closer until my chest is against his. He puts one of his hands on my neck, firm and strong, and forces me to look up at him. "He didn't take your face in his hands?"

I shake my head just barely again. My breath is ragged, and Jonny's is, too.

"He didn't push your hair back from your sweet face?" His voice gets softer and softer. I feel the heat of his chest going up and down against my taut breasts. I hear no sound apart from him, not even my own erratic pulse. I feel nothing other than him in front of me, around me, and on me. His other hand grabs my waist tightly, and just the feel of it there sets all of my internal organs on fire. My knees buckle for a second, but Jonny is holding me up.

"He didn't pull you into him?" Jonny yanks my body so close to his I can feel his breath on my lips.

"N-n-n-no."

"I'm nervous, too, Sandy. Why am I so nervous?" I can almost feel his lips on mine as he whispers the words. I let out a whimper. He tightens his hold on my neck and my hip in response. "He didn't pull your perfect lips onto his?" Jonny inhales a shaky breath, and I can't think or see or hear or smell or observe anything. I'm lost in a haze of nerves and anticipation, until—

Buzzzzz

Buzzzzz

Buzzzzz

"Shit." He pulls out his phone, and we both look down at the screen, smacking our foreheads together.

LAYLA

I jump back as we both say, "Ow."

I...

We...

How...

We almost just...

"Shit, Sandy, I'm—" Jonny takes a step toward me.

"You should go," I say, sounding much less shaky than I feel.

He needs to leave. He has a girlfriend. He has the "love of his life." He shouldn't be here. My hands form fists when I realize I almost became a cheater and almost turned Jonny into one, too.

And why is he touching me like this now?

Talking to me this way *now*?

When I finally feel confident. When I finally feel like I belong, like things make sense. When I finally have a wonderful man who sees me, who wants me, who appreciates me as I am. Wade wanted me *before* the makeover. He admired me *before* the stupid dating lessons. *Before* new clothes.

Jonny didn't.

Jonny didn't!

"Sandy, can we at least talk about this?"

"No! Just g-go, Jonny. Go back to Layla." I spit out the words. I'm shaking with frustration and other emotions I can't even sort through. I am overwhelmed.

"And you'll go back to *Wade*?" He sounds angry, too. This pushes me from irritation into rage. It is not fair or logical for Jonny to be upset in this situation! He is the one that is eight years too late!

I move to open the door for him. I don't look him in the eyes. "Yes."

Jonny hesitates, staring at me. I know he's willing me to look up at him, so he can change my mind. So he can talk this through until he feels better. Until he can get all of his words out. But I don't look up.

He storms out. Even though I see him start to turn back in the hall, I slam the door. I stomp to the kitchen to find the Benadryl I sometimes take to help me sleep when I am overstimulated. I take one, climb into my bed, and immediately start reading a fantasy novel.

I focus all my energy on reading comprehension. I need the escape. I need sleep. I cannot think or feel any more tonight. Whatever else is going to happen with me or Jonny, it will have to wait until tomorrow.

CHAPTER 18

Saturday is a whirlwind. In my bad-double-date stupor, I forgot to begin packing. This upcoming week is spring break, so I'm headed to California to see Lee and Avery. I convinced Jenn to join me. I pack too many of my new tops and jumpers into my case. Jenn is texting me every few seconds, but I welcome the distraction from my thoughts of last night.

The awkward date.

The not-kiss good night.

The second not-kiss that almost ruined everything. It was early this morning that I realized how unfortunate a kiss with Jonny would have been. Not only would our friendship have been altered permanently, his relationship with Layla would have been also. The relationship with *his* longtime love, *his* childhood crush. Jonny would never forgive me for that. And despite my frustration with him, I don't think I could bear that. A life without Jonny Canton for a best friend.

That doesn't mean I know what to do now.

Other than pack as quickly as possible for my flight this evening.

Before leaving, I thank Wade for a great night and remind him of my trip. He tells me he'll think of me, miss me, and can't wait for spring break to be over. I say I agree with him on two out of three.

Jenn and I make it onto the plane and across the country. She is funny and fun and makes the traveling hustle and bustle much more bearable. Avery and Lee meet us at the airport and take us to get fresh sushi right away. Lee swears to Jenn that there is absolutely nothing like fresh California sushi. Later, Jenn agrees.

Over dinner, after much cajoling, I tell my girlfriends everything that's happened. They go through a litany of emotions, responses, and occasional cuss words. By the time we make it to my old apartment, all three girls are solidly on Team Wade. Lee has even declared she's not sure we can remain friends if I continue a friendship with Jonny. She says he is holding me back from my goddess within. I tell her to point out said goddess on an anatomy chart. We all laugh.

It's only at midnight Oklahoma time that I hear from Jonny. I'm unsure I even want to open the text, but I can't stand not knowing what he's thinking and feeling.

Jonny: I propose an experiment.

Me: ?

Jonny: Let's carry on as if last night never happened.

Jonny: Desired outcome: I don't lose my best friend.

Me: It's a valid idea.

Jonny: Our friendship is the best thing in my life. I can't lose you, Sand.

Me: Terms?

Jonny: Neither of us speaks of it ever again.

Me: I have an additional parameter.

Jonny: I agree!

Me: You don't know what it is.

Jonny: Whatever it is, I'm fine with it!

Me: My addition was no more double dates.

Jonny: Hell yes, absolutely!!

Jonny: Can we begin?

Me: Yes.

Jonny: [Animate Gif Spring Break Baby]

Jonny: Let me guess, you're studying.

Me: Nope! On a trip.

Jonny: What? Where? With who? When? How?

Me: Back in California. I'll send you some pics.

Jonny: OK.

Jonny: Nite, Sandy.

Me: Good night.

The girls and I enjoy every second of spring break. Jenn and Avery are the bubbly, outgoing yin to the introverted yang provided by Lee and me. We talk to the point of exhaustion, for the latter party, anyway. But the discussions are helpful.

Case in point: I should not publicly declare Wade as my boyfriend until after the semester is over. We are not yet deep or serious; better to press pause now than to be caught kissing in the hallway. I am fairly sure that would never happen, given Wade's restraint, but Jenn claims he "noticeably eye fucks me during his lectures."

When I arrive back to my apartment on Saturday, I feel refreshed, happy, clear, and complete. Jonny has sent me silly messages all week, with two reminders about how I am his best friend whom he cannot live without. My face actually ached from smiling on Thursday, when Jonny was bored on a trip and sent at least one message an hour.

Wade has sent sweet messages, too, but I know what I need to say to him. I have a plan. And now, with the addition of Jenn who is actually at school with me, I have a real circle of strong girlfriends.

I truly feel Peak Sandra.

Wade arrives at my apartment a couple hours after I do.

"Gorgeous. I missed you." He pulls me in for a few kisses. One, two, three.

"Hello yourself," I say, still a bit dizzy that such a gorgeous, intelligent man wants to be my boyfriend.

"I brought tacos."

"We need to talk."

We both say the words at the same time.

"Shit, that's never good." Wade sets the bag down on the counter.

I take a deep breath and remember the speech my girls coached me through. "In undergrad, there was a girl in one of my c-c-c-classes."

"Hey." Wade puts his hands on my arms and rubs gently.

"Let me get this out."

"All right." He puts his hands down.

"This girl dated one of our professors. He is a young guy and single. And none of us think they actually broke any rules. But it still became a huge deal. For the student."

"Ah."

I continue, "Her reputation was ripped apart, her grades were questioned, and she couldn't even finish out the semester. Meanwhile, the professor was t-t-totally unaffected."

"Sandra, no one in their right mind would question the merit of your grades. You're in the top of *every* class, not just mine. And I'm not even a professor." His hand is back on my arm. His eyes are pleading and his voice is soft.

"I appreciate that, but people are not in their right minds when it comes to hot TAs. School is like a small town and gossip spreads like a bacteria in dark, moist, ideal conditions. You can't argue that."

His face has a hint of a smile. "So what are you saying?"

"I'm saying we hold off until after the semester, just a couple of months."

He looks at me, then down at his feet. We stand in silence for a few minutes.

"While you were gone, I had time to think." He swallows. "I decided I want to focus on the spine."

"Neurology."

He nods. "I applied for residency here, of course, but it's not guaranteed."

I nod.

We have very loosely discussed going through the end of orthopedic residency together. That has been the extent of our conversation about his future. I knew it was looming but didn't want to assume he was imagining me as a part of the next five years of his life.

"I don't want to hold off, Sandra." He looks in my eyes. "I want you to be my girlfriend right now, and the rest of the semester, the summer...but it might be a wise idea to wait until after match day, when we find out where I'm going."

We talk about his goals, what the next few months will be like, and how crazy the hours will be once his residency starts. We eat and talk, and he holds my hand on the couch. When he pauses by the door a couple hours later, he kisses me on each cheek and on my forehead. One, two, three.

He leaves, and I no longer have a boyfriend. I am no longer dating. I don't feel very upset at the realization. My phone buzzes with a photo of Jonny with a turtle in a reptile store. The text with the photo reads, "Almost took this mini dinosaur home with me. Turtles Rule Bugs Drool."

I smile and start to unpack my clothes.

For now, I am content.

CHAPTER 19

Jonny: WHERE ARE YOU????

I laugh out loud at the message. The end of my semester was an intense blur. I pushed myself to make near-perfect scores on my finals to make up for some periods of distraction earlier in the semester. Dating is not good for one's grades.

I still get to see Wade for coffee semi-regularly, as friends. His gaze lingers and our his hugs are held for a long time, but we are committed. He's just starting his residency and needs to get settled before we can discuss any next steps.

I get a small slice of summer before my much more intense second year of med school begins, so I intend to enjoy it. Normally, that would mean reading and attempting to master some of next semester's materials early, but Jenn has different ideas. As does Jonny.

After my tests, she and I went to California to see the girls for a few weeks and celebrate my twenty-first birthday. When we got back, we found a new apartment together, which will hopefully be a good thing. I love her, but she is a talker and enjoys togetherness almost as much as I enjoy my solitude. I hope we'll find a balance.

Jonny's travel schedule picked up in June, so with all of those variables, it's been a couple months since we've been able to get together. Tonight, I promised Jonny I would be at the Canton family fireworks show if he promised to show up early. He agreed on the condition that I would stay until at least after the fireworks were over. I said we'd see how it goes.

The memory of last year is still vivid in my mind. Though things are much different tonight. We text now. Every day. He never mentions Layla. I never mention Wade, but there hasn't been anything to mention about him since spring break.

My phone buzzes once more, and I laugh again.

Approximately twenty seconds ago, he said he had arrived at the country club.

Jonny: .....

Me: I'm getting in my car and I will not text while driving. See you there.

Jonny: I am not going to take the lack of exclamation marks in your text messages personally...

I pull my solid red dress down a bit as I head up the country club steps. Jenn said I *had* to get a few of these sporty tank dresses because they were *made for my twiggy body.* I agreed because I can wear my Converse with them.

My wavy hair blows all over the place, so I push my sunglasses back as a headband. My hair is longer and even more unruly, but when I went to Heather for fresh highlights, she said long beach waves were "totally in." I didn't tell her that I would be keeping them long after they were totally *out.*

I look around the space for Jonny, stopping habitually every time my eyes find a petite figure with perfectly symmetrical curves and long, straight, blond hair. I also look at every pod of people in a circle, knowing he might be in their center, telling a funny story. But I don't find him.

"Sandy."

I look to my right and see him there, though I didn't even recognize his voice. He's not smiling, which is odd. Instead, he's biting his lip. His whole body is tense, actually, as if he's about to jump into a fight. His hands are even fisted at his sides.

"Hey." I smile and walk toward him, and his hands relax. But his shoulders don't. I realize as I walk that he keeps looking at my legs. The dress is short, but legs are legs. He's seen mine a million times. He hasn't stepped in my direction yet. "Uh, do I get a hug?"

"Yeah, of course." He shakes his head a bit and then wraps his bulky arms around me. I relax into the hug I know so well, preparing for it to end prematurely, as always. But it doesn't. Instead, Jonny inhales for a minute, like he's breathing through our embrace.

He squeezes me tightly and picks me up off the ground. I laugh in surprise at being lifted like I weigh nothing. Jonny grits out, "Girl genius, home at last." His voice is so strained, maybe I weigh a bit more than nothing.

He sets me down and releases his lock around my back, but his hands land on my waist. They stay there. The warmth of them through the thin athletic fabric of my dress sends a shock-wave through my nervous system.

He grins like he's up to something. "Hey."

"Hey?" My head tilts at his odd behavior.

He clears his throat and lets go of me. "Hungry?"

"Sure."

"Well, c'mon then." He leads me by the hand through the crowd. People wave to him and a few say hello to me, but he doesn't stop. In fact, he links my fingers with his like he did on our fake date months ago. My pulse quickens.

We load up our plates with typical barbecue fare, but I'm suddenly not that hungry. We're at a table with a few acquaintances who start to chat with Jonny as soon as we sit down. I notice he doesn't eat right away, either. Then he stretches an arm to rest on the back of my chair, with his thumb touching my bare shoulder. Jonny's voice, hands, fingers...it's all too stimulating. I start to sweat, even though we're inside in the air conditioning. Jonny politely bows out of the table conversation and turns to me but doesn't look at me.

"So, I know you moved in with Jenn... What's Wade think of that?"

I did not expect this question. "What?"

Jonny raises his voice a tiny bit. "I just mean, you know, did he want you to move in with him? Or are you guys not that serious yet?"

"Oh. We, uh, aren't together." Jonny's eyes shoot to mine. I realize with how I said it, it seems like I got dumped. "I didn't want people to talk, since he was my TA, and he is starting his residency, so."

Jonny takes a big gulp of his lemonade.

He leans much closer into me so he can speak softly. "It's so loud in here. Wanna go eat somewhere else?"

"Okay." I realize we're about to leave his party early, like I did last year. "Wait, what about Layla?"

"Oh, I don't think she's here."

"But isn't she coming?"

"I don't know."

Before I can ask what that means, he leads me through the crowd. Again he's linked our fingers together, pulling me through the crowd like he's being chased. I catch some of the glances as we pass. Jonny is holding my hand in front of all of his family and friends. He continues until we're at his truck, where he lets go to open the passenger door for me.

He gets in next to me and starts the obnoxious engine. "Carino's okay? There's that one a couple blocks from here?"

"Sure."

On the short drive over, he glances at me so often I worry about us crashing.

"What? Did I spill something on myself?" It would be *on brand* for me, as Avery says.

"Shit, no." Jonny shifts in his seat. "Sorry."

"Sorry for what?"

"Staring, I guess." He doesn't look at me at all as he answers. I look away, too, feeling my epidermis strive to match the red of my dress. We're at the restaurant in no time. I climb out of the truck, eager for fresh air. I don't find any, though, since I'm in Tulsa in July.

"Dammit, Sandy." I turn to face him as he rounds the back of the truck. "I told you to let me get your door for you."

"That's just on dates." I say it almost as a question.

He deflates a little bit, less angry but also less...something else. "Oh. Right."

We head inside, and I almost don't even notice the hostess obviously ogling Jonny. I'm used to it. There are plenty of former football players in this state, but Jonny looks like he still plays. Add the teal eyes and perfect features, I can't blame the girl.

"This is better," he says after the hostess and server leave. His eyes sparkle at me. "Now I can hear you tell me all about your tests and California and everything else."

And I do. And I ask him all about the new franchises, the boring board meetings, and the latest blunders by Robot Rob. Both of us barely touch our food, but that could be because we're talking and laughing so much.

"Are you sure about cutting people open, though?" Jonny asks after dinner with a shudder.

I nod with a sure smile. "Absolutely."

"And all that pressure? It looks really intense on TV."

"I like pressure. You know that. I can sit alone with a puzzle and a timer, remember?"

He grimaces. "That was a long Saturday for me...Saturdays. Plural." I laugh. He starts to laugh, too, but stops and adds on a thought. "We're such opposites. You wanted to be alone and work on your brain teasers in silence. I didn't want to be alone or in silence, ever. Still don't. Not often, anyway."

A strange heaviness settles between us. It's an odd sensation. After all, it's not as if we haven't realized we're polar opposites many times. He's teased me incessantly about any and all manner of differences.

A loud boom clears the air around our table.

Jonny's eyes go so wide I think his pupils may have disagreed. "Shit, Sand, the fireworks! We gotta get back over there!"

Had we really talked for four hours straight?! I suppose we always could do that. We giggle as we rush out of the restaurant, literally running to his truck. He yells at me to get buckled as he's already peeling out of the parking lot. It is dramatic, even for him. We keep up the dramatics until we reached the edge of the big lawn.

He grabs my hand again. The feel of my thin fingers feels different in his hot, thick hands. Maybe because it's after dark, under a spray of sparkles. His family always sits in the same central spot, but he doesn't lead me over to them. Instead, he finds a spot out of the way, against one of the club's exterior walls.

He leans against the wall and pulls me into him.

"Jonny." He knows what I mean as I say it.

He puts his hands around me from behind. It's so hot, as if his chest lights up my back with sparks to rival the sky above. It is the most glorious sensation I ever felt. But I can't relax, can't think. I felt his breath in my ear before I heard his low whisper.

"Layla and I broke up, Sand."

I let out the breath I'd been holding. "When?"

"You know the night that we don't talk about?"

I nodded.

"The next morning."

I...

I...

I can't think straight. What does that mean, the next morning? He hasn't been with her these few months we've been texting, sometimes talking? He's been single? He's single now?

He's single now.

I'm single now.

He moves his thumbs against me where his hands hold me on my sides.

His words are low and hard in my ear. "Do you want me to let you go?"

I shake my head. I do not want him to let me go. That is maybe the only thought I can think in this moment.

"Then relax, Sandy. Enjoy the fireworks."

I look up with my eyes, but I don't really see the show. I can't compute all of this. Jonny is hard and hot around me, behind me, in my ear, chuckling when I startle at the loudest explosions. His arms leave me, and I start to stand up, but he yanks my hips back. Then I feel his hands on my shoulders, into my neck and...

My hair.

He's scooping my sweaty, wild mane off of my neck.

"D'you have a hairband?" His voice in my ear is altogether different than any sound I've ever heard from him. The lowness and roughness of it erupts a new sheen of sweat all over my skin. I— What did he say? He chuckles softly in a way that affects my hormones. "Sandy. Hair band." Oh! I have one on my wrist! I hand it to him.

Jonny Canton puts my hair in a bun on top of my head.

As I start to think about this, how he knows to do this, how he's so good at everything he does...

He...

Blows...

On...

My...

Neck!

I...

He...

I...

I shiver violently in his arms, which are back around me. He tightens them in response to my trembling. The finale of the show starts to a chorus of screams and horns. Jonny pushes me forward and then takes my hand. He leads me out to the parking lot.

"Let's get you out of here before the traffic gets crazy," he whispers in my ear. I think. I'm not sure I can trust my ears or eyes or any of the other senses. He walks me toward my car instead of his, and disappointment overtakes me. I don't want this night to end. I don't want to wake up from this dream to a nightmare where Jonny doesn't talk to me like this. Touch me like this. We pause at my car door. "Sand." He breaks me out of my tumbling thoughts. "Stay and hang out with me tomorrow."

"Oh, uh, I..." I try and remember what I had planned for tomorrow.

"C'mon, I'll pick you up at your parents' place and we'll go out. It'll be fun."

I smile, unable to say no to him, as always. "Ok-k-kay."

Jonny nods and turns away but then suddenly turns back. I step back into my car, my back up against the warm metal of the driver's-side door.

"Sandy, he was an idiot that night. *Wade.*" He spits the name out. "An idiot that night and any night that ended where he didn't."

I blink a few times, trying to catch my senses up with what he's saying. "...Didn't what?"

"Do this."

Jonny's hands clutch my neck, grabbing my face and pulling my mouth onto his. His lips press on mine for one frozen moment before he twists my head and...

And...

And...

Consumes...

Overtakes...

Devours...

He—

If this is kissing, I have not previously been kissed. He is the first. He is the only. His tongue...captures mine and takes it prisoner. He tastes like cinnamon gum and feels like a deep moan. All of my internal systems become overwhelmed with wet heat. I no longer feel his hands, hear the fireworks, sense the humidity in the air.

There's only Jonny.

Jonny and me, together.

Us.

He pulls away, and I let out a moan of my own. His arms release my head and move to my car, caging me in. He stares down at me, panting. I realize I'm out of breath, too.

"Don't overthink this, Sand. Go home and read your latest faerie novel and go to sleep. Then I'll pick you up tomorrow for a date. A real one. You and me. Okay?"

"Ok-k-k-kay."

"Dammit," he mutters under his breath before his mouth is on mine again. One of his hands revisits my neck, and I cling to his forearm, no longer frozen in shock. Now I'm frozen in need, in want. My other hand drops my keys in order to fist the fabric of his shirt. He groans and pulls away.

"Quit seducing me, woman! Everyone we know is walking into this parking lot right now."

"Sssss—"

"Yes. Seducing. Your beautiful brain misfiring because of me. And I'm crying uncle here, because I don't want to have my first make out session with you in front of the whole town." He pushes off of the car and releases my head. He grabs my keys and puts them back in my hand. "Home, book, sleep."

"Have you always b-been this bossy?"

"Yes. Good night, Sandy." He smiles and backs up a few more steps. I hate the distance. "Go!"

"Okay! Geez!" I raise my voice back at him, surprising myself.

Annoying as it is, I obey his orders. Even down to which book, but he must've just remembered the series I am currently reading. I defy him when it comes to going to sleep, though. Instead of sleep, I relive the last hour with him over and over and over in my brain until my body finally shuts down to rest.

KELSEY HUMPHREYS

CHAPTER 20

It's morning. On a Sunday. In my parents' house. That explains the commotion downstairs at eight a.m. God apparently frowns on missing Sunday school before service. This makes me wonder how he feels about me skipping both. I sigh and decide to at least go watch the sermon online. That way I'm sort of joining my parents.

And Jonny.

Jonny.

I relive last night exactly six more times before actually going downstairs. The memory makes the lower half of my body ache. At the coffee pot, I resume my initial thought. Jonny is at church, too. But he didn't pester me to go with him. More noteworthy, he did not invite me to brunch.

He has tried to get me to resume my attendance at brunch with his family for months. Why would he stop now? He isn't with Layla. He kissed me. But does that mean he's with me? If I go to brunch with him, will everyone know we're dating? Will that make me his girlfriend? Is that what I want? Is that what he wants? I pull out my phone to turn off DND. There's already a message from him.

Jonny: Missing you at church and brunch but didn't think you'd be up for about 1.4 trillion questions. Since half the city saw us in the parking lot, make that 1.5 trillion.

Me: You were right.

Jonny: As soon as I can make a break for it, I'm coming to get you. Don't dress up too much for our date. Something you can walk around in.

Me: Now I require more details, please.

Jonny: Too bad.

Me: [angry emoji]

Jonny: Quit texting me while I'm in church! [praying hands emoji]

A few hours later, Jonny is at my parents' door for our date. He's casually dressed in a teal polo shirt and shorts, but holding a single long-stemmed red rose. To say the scene is surreal would be an understatement.

For the first time in our lives, Jonny slowly and obviously checks me out. I chose my shortest short-shorts and a slouchy, off-the-shoulder shirt. My lacy bralette strap shows, but it was either that or no bra at all, and the second option did not feel Peak Sandra. I piled my hair up on top of my head because it's hot. And because Jenn claims necks are sensual. After last night, I agree.

Jonny's charming smile fades as he looks me up and down.

"I'm not sure about those shorts, Sandy."

I look down, too. "Why?"

"There are people, other guys out there." He motions over his shoulder with a thumb.

I look behind him. "Out where?"

"Anywhere. Everywhere. In the world. Did you bring any longer shorts?"

I sigh. "No. I really have this or the dress from last night."

"This! Definitely this." He makes a move to step in, but I stop him.

"Shouldn't my date say something nice about my attire?"

"I just said I liked your shorts."

I scoff. "That is not what you said! You asked me to change!"

"Because you look too hot, dammit!" he yells as he pulls on the back of his neck with one hand, seemingly as confused as I am.

"You want me to look less hot." I mean the statement as a question.

"No. Forget I said that about your shorts."

I shake my head. "Lllllayla went out with you in much shhhh-horter, tighter shorts. Explain what you mean, please."

"Mother f—" he mutters before taking a breath and turning to face me. "Sandy. You look fine. Let's just go."

I put the rose on my parents' entry table and then pull their door closed behind me. I type in the code on the lock and follow Jonny down the stairs.

I no longer feel Peak Sandra.

Jonny's words have always affected me more than anyone else's. He's never really commented on my appearance at all growing up, other than to say he liked my new glasses or new shoes. And I suppose until now maybe there wasn't much to comment on. The thought makes me sad and embarrassed. He did say I was hot, didn't he? But then he said I looked *fine.*

"Sandy." I look up. Jonny is standing in front of the passenger door of his truck. I have been standing in front of him staring at my feet. How long have we been standing here? Jonny sighs as he cups his hands around my face. "You are beautiful. You look way better than fine. I meant what I said. Your shorts look really hot, and I don't want any other guys to see them, okay?"

I nod, but my thoughts still swirl.

He grins at me. "I'm going to shut up that big brain of yours now."

"Wha—"

Before I can finish the very short word, Jonny's lips are on mine. His tongue takes over my mouth. I enjoy the invasion. I tilt my head to kiss him back bigger and harder. He moans and sucks on my tongue before pulling away.

He pushes a hard, closed-mouth kiss to my lips. "Are"—*kiss*—"you"—*kiss*—"ready"—*kiss*—"now?"

"Mhmm," I say. I think. My eyes are still closed.

"C'mon, let's progress past making out outside one of our cars." Jonny laughs, and I manage to open my eyes. I climb into his truck, and we start heading to our destination. He turns on Frankie Valli and the Four Seasons and turns up the volume. We both sing along.

Soon we pull into an old parking lot in what looks like a very questionable area. Jonny's smile is trouble when he puts the truck in park. "Has your putt-putt game gotten any better?" He points to the sign.

"Celebration Station, really?"

"C'mon, this was one of our favorite places. I am still a master at ski-ball. I bet they've got a giant stuffed ladybug or spider or some kind of insect in there, and I'm gonna get it for you."

I roll my eyes as he helps me down from his truck. "This was *your* favorite place."

"I'll kiss you in the photo booth."

That forces my facial muscles to pull back into a smile. It also makes my head spin. Did he know I'd always wanted that? Was I so obvious our whole lives? And if I was, why did he reject me over and over again? When I concede, Jonny's grin is victorious, and he gloats about it.

But he does kiss me in the photo booth and in the arcade. And while driving a go-cart. And when he sulks after losing to me at air hockey. And after he wins enough tickets at ski-ball to get me a small stuffed ladybug. It was not the biggest prize, but I convinced him I did not actually want an eight-foot-tall stuffed banana.

After Celebration Station, he takes me to Sonic. He smiles again, this time not having to explain himself. The day he got his driver's license, he took me to Sonic after school. In the summer, we would go there just to go somewhere and do something that wasn't sitting at his house or trying not to faint in the heat by the pool.

"Don't worry, just drinks. I'll take you for a real dinner."

He does take me to dinner. At Red Lobster. Another inside joke pertaining to my repeated nightmares about lobsters desperate for escape. I still do not eat lobster.

Dinner flies by, like the whole day has. It's early, so Jonny suggests we go to his house. I agree, but my heart palpitates wildly at the thought. I've never been to his place. I've never been invited back to any man's home before. I'm fairly certain I know what it will look like, but what will happen inside? What does Jonny expect? What does he want?

"Brainy," Jonny whispers in my ear. Somehow we are already standing outside his front door. We didn't pull into his garage, I guess? Where has my mind been? I look up at him as he closes both of his hands around mine, which are seizing up with nerves.

He gives me a squeeze. "Here's what's going to happen. I'm going to take you inside, give you a little tour, set you down on the couch, and then I'm going to kiss the shit out of you. Then I'm going to fix you some tea and you're going to drive back to the city. Does that sound good to you?"

"Uh huh," I manage to whisper.

Jonny opens the door to a shining, modern, seemingly brand new home. It has to be a few years old, but it looks as if it was pulled from a magazine. Except for the mess. As I expected, the place is clean but cluttered. I can tell Jonny's mom had helped with the decorating. Family photos, OU paraphernalia, and Canton Cards merchandise are everywhere.

After the gleaming kitchen, dining, and living area, Jonny shows me the clearly unused guest bedroom and his office. The desk and shelves are almost completely covered in papers and supplies, indicating Jonny actually works here. It would be tidy otherwise. The thought makes me smile.

Until I see it next to the monitor.

A small framed photo of Layla. Seeing her there, perfectly coiffed in an OU Cheer uniform, my brain works like it's solving a game of memory. She's actually all throughout the house. I didn't notice, or perhaps blocked out, how many group photos she's in, how many photos there are of the two of them. Jonny is talking, of course, so he doesn't catch where my eyes have landed. I move quickly out of the room, rubbing my hand on my chest in an attempt to soothe a physical ache there.

Jonny's room is surprisingly well-kept and sparse. He must not spend much time in here. Plus, he shows me, there's a giant closet where he can be totally lazy with his clothes. Suits, jeans, flip flops, hats, they're everywhere.

He laughs at my reaction. "Maryanne, my housekeeper, she comes on Tuesdays."

I let out a small giggle, trying to relax. I walk back out into his room and see another small frame next to what's obviously his side of the bed. My hand goes to my chest again. I am unsure how much more of Framed Layla I can take. But I notice there's no blond in the frame. I dare to walk over.

Jonny's voice is warm and gentle. "I love that picture. It's moved from my old room at home to every room I've had."

It's us. A shot taken at his last home football game in eighth grade. I was twelve and he was about to turn fifteen. He's smiling at the camera like he's the king of the universe, which was how he acted at the time. He was the captain of the varsity middle school football team, after all. I'm gazing up at him through my thick glasses, smiling wildly. Our arms are around each other, but the way I am looking at him, and he at the camera, explains so much.

I rub my chest again and set the small frame down. On his nightstand. He keeps a photo of me, of us, on his nightstand. Emotions fire through all my pathways, neurological and otherwise. My eyes start to leak big, confused tears.

"Sandy? Hey." He closes his arms around me so tight he cuts off some of my circulation. And airflow. It is an effective way to stop my crying. But I do cough in an effort to breathe. He loosens his hold and pulls back to look at me. "I'm sorry, Sand."

"Fffff." I sniff and huff in frustration. Emotions muddle everything!

"For taking so long," he whispers. Then he kisses me gently. I relax into him but don't move my arms to hold him, because I can't move them. He feels me shifting. When he lets me go, I step back. I'm still unsure, unsettled. "What?" Jonny stares at me, hands on his hips, frustrated. "Just tell me what you're thinking!"

I glare at him and then storm out of his room. I walk to the office and grab Layla's photo. He comes up behind me, and I turn to hand it to him.

"Damn, I'm sorry. I didn't even realize this was still there. I didn't even see it anymore."

I try to be clear. "Shhhhe's everywhere."

"She's not."

"She is!"

"Okay, I'll go through and take all the pictures down, then." He huffs back at me. He waits for me to nod, to absolve him. As if his magnanimous gesture of removing her photos will make everything better. "C'mon, Sandy, you were with Wade, too. It's not like you have no past, no guys before me." Tears threaten again at how wrong he is. There was no one before him or after him. Only ever Jonny.

His hands cradle my face again. I close my eyes and hear his soft words travel straight to my heart. "Sandy, sweetheart, tell me what to do. Quit thinking so much and just tell me how to fix it."

I open my eyes and stare into all that teal. His face is so earnest and maybe even scared? He looks ten years old again. His thumb caresses my jawline. But it's his worried eyes that win me over.

"You mmmentioned kissing the shhh—"

He kisses the words from me. He picks me up in a quick motion and wraps my legs around his waist while still kissing me. I feel as though I am just trying to keep up with him, to not faint. He's so intense and big and warm and everywhere.

He plops down forcefully, with me in his lap. Our kiss breaks with the motion, and I freeze in a moment of terror and delight. I'm straddling Jonny. On his couch. In his living room, in his house. I smile, and he smiles, too. He rubs his hot palms up and down my bare thighs.

"Damn those shorts." He chuckles, and I relax down further onto him. He looks down at his lap and then back up to me and curses under his breath. His voice comes out breathy and tight. "I'm nervous, Sandy."

"Mmme, too." He leans up and kisses me eagerly with his tongue and then falls back about the couch entirely prematurely. His hands slide up to my waist, then back to grab my backside, hard, which overwhelms my body with arousal. No hands have ever rubbed me like this.

Jonny groans. "Yeah. It's probably good you stay on top of me."

I disagree. I don't know what to do. I should not be in charge here!

I gather some strength and direct it to my vocal cords. "I've never sat like this."

His face goes slack, and his whole body tenses. "Wait. Are you...have you never..."

"I have. It just...wasn't like this."

He relaxes and pulls me closer to him. He adjusts underneath me, and I observe that I am not the only aroused party. My eyes widen when I estimate the size of...him.

He sees my surprise. Surprise or perhaps terror. My brain is not fully functional anymore.

"Hey." He's whispering again. "It's just me. You and me, Sandy. Just us."

I barely hear my voice come out in reply. "I don't know what to do."

"Whatever you want." He continues to rub my thighs with his rough hands. There is no rhythm or pattern to his strokes and squeezes on my skin. I want more of his skin, I realize.

"I want you to take your shirt off."

Jonny smiles wide. "Yes, ma'am." He whips off his shirt and leans up toward me, kissing me with small strokes that feel like nudges. My hands fall onto his bare chest, and my eyes fly open.

I...

He...

He...

My response is unexpected. I've seen him shirtless before. But I've never felt him. I move my hands over all of his skin. His shoulders are so hard. His chest has more short, light brown hair than I remember. I pull my fingers down through it, to his abs. He has always had abs like a model. Like an athlete. He groans as I stare at him. I can't organize my thoughts, other than the word more. *More, more, more.* I'm frozen with it, my processes stalled out by it.

"Sandy, stop thinking so much and—"

I whip my loose top over my head in a moment of realization. More skin. My skin and his skin.

"Okay, keep thinking. Thinking is great. Thinking is fine." Jonny's muttering is almost incoherent. His hands go up to my sides, gripping into my ribs with force. His eyes look at all my skin, coming back to my small amount of cleavage again and again. He licks his lips and grips me tighter.

"Kiss me now." I pull him up, and he doesn't hesitate. Our chests collide along with our mouths. Jonny's hands slide along my back and up into my hair and down my arms. We kiss for an eternity. Then his mouth leaves mine and ventures to my jaw-line, my neck.

He is kissing my neck.

Thoughts.

Happiness.

Sweat.

Wetness. So much wetness.

His mouth moves to my ear. "You're perfect, Sandy. So perfect."

My body shakes at his words, totally overloaded. His kisses return to my mouth with fierceness. My trembling continues, even though I will it to stop. Mind-over-matter is a scientific fact that is categorically failing me in this moment. Jonny pulls his head back but clutches my body to his.

"I want to do this all night, but it's getting late, and you have a long drive." He picks me up and sets me on the coffee table. He slowly and carefully puts my shirt back on me, kissing me as he does it. "Let me get you that tea."

My body calms as I watch him in the kitchen from my perch on his coffee table. I am surprised that he has tea on hand. He fixes it for me, watches me drink, and talks about his week. I listen. Then he deposits me at my car with more hard, breath-stealing kisses.

"Turn up your fancy orchestra music and drive, Sand." He taps the hood of my car, and I focus on my task. I smile the entire drive home. At one point, I burst out in uncontrolled giggles that do not make sense. My body is releasing adrenaline, I surmise. I make it back to my apartment just before midnight. I don't sleep a wink.

CHAPTER 21

Jonny: This is a FANCY date! Very swanky, so dress up. =)

Me: Ok.

Jonny: This has been the longest week of my life so I'll probably
be there early. I can't wait to see you!

Me: I can't wait, either.

Jonny: I need some punctuation, please.

Me: Just hurry up and get here! !!!!!!!!

Jonny: [heart emoji]

"O pera?!" I can't believe it. "You hate this kind of thing."
"I really, really do." Jonny beams at me. "But it's worth it to see you all dressed up. Have I told you you look incredible?"

"You did."

"What about beautiful, did I say that?"

I nod and blush for the hundredth time this week. My epidermis is exhausted from Jonny's compliments, shirtless selfies, dirty jokes, and detailed descriptions of how much he liked my breasts in my bra last Sunday and how much he can't wait to see more of me. I worry he is a little bit out of control.

But I am out of control myself. I even sent him a photo of my cleavage in a push-up bra, after much coaching from Jenn. She added, however, that she is not yet on Team Jonny but rather feels strongly that sending sexy photos is a Peak Sandra activity. I shook when I hit send. Still there I was, sending sexy selfies.

It's been the best week of my entire life.

Jonny holds me tightly around the waist as we wait at the bar for champagne. He is obvious about checking me out, repeatedly. I borrowed a sparkly black halter dress from Jenn. The tight fit and choker neckline doesn't provide any enhancements for my chest, but the dress has a high slit that makes my legs look sexy—like they belong to someone else. Jonny seems to appreciate the aforementioned slit.

He leans down and coats my exposed neck with his breath. "I'm going to shift you in front of me so I can grab your ass now. Don't squeak."

He moves me. He grabs me.

I squeak.

He throws his head back and laughs before tucking me into himself. We shuffle along in the line like that, his chest behind my back. This line is my new favorite place in all the world. *Sorry, Museum of Science and Industry.*

We enjoy the first act from wonderful seats that I'm sure Jonny paid highly for. He holds my hand throughout the entire show, sometimes kissing my knuckles. I can hardly look way from the beautiful scene on the stage, but when I do, Jonny is watching me. I blush all over again.

At intermission, Jonny leaves me in line at the bar to go to the restroom. Joel and Steven, two fellow med students, notice me. I give them a wave, and they saunter over. We engage in small talk about summer for a moment until Joel shifts the conversation to the first act we've just watched. We all disagree on our translations of a few key pieces of Italian.

I laugh at Joel's terrible attempt to speak the language. As I do, Jonny's giant arm slides around my waist. I smile at up at him, but he is not smiling. He looks like perhaps he just experienced stomach trouble in the restroom.

"Hey, guys, I'm Jonny." He extends a hand. I realize I have missed a social convention.

"Sorry, yes, this is Joel and Steven. They are second years with me."

Joel adjusts his glasses. "Almost. Second year hasn't technically started yet."

"Right!" I laugh. Joel and Steven smile, but there is tension in their faces. Jonny's grip on my hip becomes almost painful. "We were just arguing over the Italian. In the shhhhow," I say, hoping to ease whatever it is that is making Jonny act irrationally.

He relaxes and kisses the side of my head. "Gotcha. Nice meeting you." Jonny's clipped words are a clear dismissal. My friends eye each other, then me, then turn and walk away.

"Jonny? Are you all right?"

"Yup." He doesn't look at me. We get our drinks and go back to our seats, and he keeps my hand in his. But he doesn't watch me during the second act like he did in the first. When he leads me out into the aisle after the curtain closes, he remains tense. I watch him closely, trying to decipher what he's thinking or feeling. My mind gets distracted by his raw appeal, from his hard jaw to his perfect, tight suit. To the teal tie I know he wore just for me.

"Jonny?"

He finally looks at me. "Yeah?"

I lean into him so I don't have to shout the words. "You're the hottest man I've ever seen. You always have b-b-been."

He smiles and stops walking. There's a crowd around us, but he doesn't seem to notice or care as he grabs my head and my waist and pulls me in to kiss me so hard I...

...

Cheers break into my senses, which were completely blocked out. Someone is clapping for our kiss. Someone yells, "Get a room!" before laughing at their own predictable joke. He tucks my hand into his arm and escorts me into the lobby as if we didn't just make a public spectacle of ourselves. His grin gives his obvious pride away. He loves a good spectacle.

"Jonny?" A voice calls to us. "And Sandra? Sandra *Hayes*?"

Rob the Robot approaches us with his fiancé, Beth. They look gorgeous, if a bit stiff.

Jonny's voice is tense. "I didn't know you were coming tonight."

Rob nods. "Had a business dinner. Wait." His face contorts. "Are you guys here *together*?"

"Yup." Jonny shifts his attention. "Beth, you've met Sandy before, right?"

"Right, hi." Beth gives me a polite smile that I return.

"Oh, Sandra, don't tell me you fell for this moron's cheap tricks after all this time. Aren't you a genius? You gotta know you're way too good for him." Rob gestures at his brother, as if it's not clear who he meant.

Beth grabs her fiancé's arm. "Rob!"

"Uh. Sorry. I mean, it's the truth, but regardless, Sandra, you look lovely. Always a pleasure to see you." He bows awkwardly like we're in a different era of time, then turns and pulls Beth away.

"Ssstill a t-t-t-urd," I say, flustered and wishing I could have kept Jonny from that, protected him from his oldest, meanest bully.

Jonny adjusts his tie with a grunt. "You got that right."

We drive in silence. I watch Jonny drive, and he doesn't notice my staring. His mind must be racing feverishly if his mouth can't keep up. It's uncanny to see him quiet for so long.

"Thanks for taking me to see that." My voice comes out sounding crunchy. Odd description, but fitting.

"You bet, Sandygirl."

He parks in a small public lot near my apartment and walks around to get my door. He opens it and watches me turn and extend my leg through the long slit up the side of my dress. He eyes my leg but also my shoe. He puts his hands on my hips to stop me from jumping down.

"Sandra Hayes. How long have you had those Converse?"

I frown, surprised at his question. "Six years."

Do my scuffed old shoes ruin the dress's effects?

Does he like my shoes? Or dislike them? Or...

"I love that you wore those shoes with that dress. It's just so... you."

I smile down at him, and he grabs my foot in his left hand and brings his right hand to grip my calf.

"How about sexy? Did I tell you you look sexy as hell tonight?"

I nod. My smile fades and my breath quivers as he moves his right hand up the slit of my dress. My entire body leaps to attention, every hair follicle becoming a bump.

"Those shorts last week, this slit...your long legs are gonna kill me, Sand." He reaches his left hand to my hip and moves in closer to where I sit. My right hand moves to his left shoulder. His voice changes. "Guess this is a nice way to go, though." His hand moves up thigh, into my skirt, right to the edge of my underwear. His hand stops, but his thumb caresses the inside of my thigh slowly.

"Look at me, Sand." His teal eyes look navy blue in the dim light. His voice is a deep whisper. "I want to make you feel as good as you look." His thumb brushes up against my center.

I feel myself turn crimson, for multiple glaring reasons. "N-n-no one's ever..."

Jonny is surprised. "No one's ever done this?" His thumb tucks my underwear out of the way and continues its caress on my skin. I shake my head. "Do you want me to stop?" I shake my head and squeeze my eyes closed.

"Sandy, look at me." I do. His eyes are hooded but intense. "It's just us, okay?"

I nod again. Jonny shifts his hand and pulls me closer to him so I am just barely sitting on the edge of the seat of the car. He hooks his fingers into my underwear to move them further out of his way. His eyes stay locked on mine as his fingers move to barely trace the edges of what must surely be the hottest, wettest area of my whole body. "No one's ever done this?"

I shake my head again, growing dizzy. I feel my pulse there where his fingers rub. All of my blood and nerves and thoughts seem to have rushed there. "What about this?" His fingers slide inside, and I... His fingers are inside me. It is a much more welcome feeling than I would have thought.

"Open your eyes, Sandy."

I didn't know they were closed.

He moves his fingers.

Pressure and dizziness.

Some kind of noise escapes me.

"You're the sexiest thing I've ever seen, you letting go with me."

More pressure. In and out and in and holyyyyy...

"Let go, sweetheart."

!!!!!

He pulls his hand away.

Kisses on my neck.

Jonny.

Us.

He moans in my ear. "Let's go inside."

I am suddenly aware of what just happened, outside, in a parking lot.

"Jonny! We..." He shuts the door with a proud look on his face. "Nobody saw, Sand. I checked."

I put my head in my free hand while he leads me to my apartment with the other. "Sorry, I just couldn't wait. It was that dress." He shrugs and laughs, and I realize he has my tiny sparkly clutch in his other hand. I had forgotten I even had a purse with me.

I forgot my own name. I forgot to breathe.

When we get into my apartment and shut the door, Jonny is panting.

He puts his hands on my waist. "Jenn?"

"Gone."

His mouth is on mine almost instantly. He grabs my hips and then my rear, talking into my neck. "That was the hottest thing I've ever seen. You make me crazy. We just did that in a parking lot! Shit, I love that truck now, Sandy. I'm going to have to move into that truck. Can you be with a man who lives in his truck?"

Jonny is losing his mind.

He walks me back into the wall by the door, kissing my breath away. He groans and shifts into me, and I realize the source of his insanity. It presses into my stomach, large and hot.

I grab it with my hand without thinking. Jonny freezes and re-leases a string of expletives under his breath. I can't contain my glee at the effect my touch has on him. I feel him flex in my hand.

My brain is a scrambled mess. "B-b-b—"

"Bedroom, yes, ma'am!"

I squeal with a laugh as he flips me into a cradle hold in one motion, then stalks to my room that he saw in our quick tour earlier. He closes my door behind him with his foot. Then at the foot of my bed he stops and puts me down.

He takes a small step back, breathing deeply. I step to him and push off his jacket. I want to see him, touch him, feel him. My hands move to his tie and help me undress him, quickly unbut-toning his shirt. When his shirt is off, he whips off his belt, pants, and socks. He stands panting in his boxer briefs, and I can't stop staring. He is the Jonny I've always known but bigger, harder, warmer, darker.

He picks me up and lays me down softly on my bed. I'm shak-ing, but so is he. His sits next to me and leans over me, moving his hands to my shoulders.

"Can I?" He puts his fingers on the buttons of the collar that hold up my dress. I nod, and as he undoes them, I move to pull the short zipper under my back. He shifts to gather the dress at my thighs and then slowly lifts it and shifts me until it's over my head and on the floor.

Jonny's eyes go up and down and all over me.

"Wow," he finally says. I can't help but respond with a smile. He leans down and kisses the edges of my smile before opening my mouth up to his and attacking me with his tongue. My body begins to move without my conscious instructions, lifting up to meet him where he hovers over me. Jonny keeps kissing me while he moves himself over me, rubbing my body's most sensitive spot.

I whimper, and Jonny moans. He kisses down my neck to my chest, exploring all over me with his tongue and even his teeth. The sensations are so debilitating I almost don't feel him slide off my underwear. But I notice the increased friction. He moves one hand to the waistband of his boxers and looks up at me. I realize from his expression that I am doing something wrong.

Tears.

I'm crying.

Jonny freezes.

He deflates.

"Shit! Sandy. I, I shouldn't have." He climbs off of me, and I try to get the words to come out. My brain is overloaded, but more than that, my heart is overflowing. This, him, us, tonight, the opera, his laugh, my dress, his truck, my bed, it's all the things I always wanted.

"We shouldn't have done this." Jonny has his pants on and is rambling. Why are his pants on? "This was a mistake."

"What?" He doesn't look at me. "Jonny?" My voice is shakier and softer than I want. I want to yell. I want to scream.

"Fuck! I'm sorry, Sand. I, we—I need to go. I can't do this."

I move off the bed and hold the dress up in front of my body. I move to stop him, but before I reach my bedroom door, I hear my apartment door slam.

Jonny's gone.

CHAPTER 22

My happy tears turn to sobs.

Jenn finds me in the hall, still sobbing, still clutching my dress to my naked body.

"Sand! What happened!" She is next to me with her arms around me in an instant. I sob harder. "Let it out. Let it all out, sister. I got you."

After an eternity, I straighten up and take a breath.

Jenn stands. "Just sit there. I'm going to get you some clothes and some water." She returns with both items. "Did he hurt you?" I shake my head. "Do you want to at least move to the couch?" I nod and manage to move with Jenn's support. My legs are like gelatin.

She notices the mess I made on the floor. "What's all this dirt?"

My entire body hurts at the memory. "He brought me a big outdoor pot of Morning Glory flowers."

"He couldn't just get you some roses like a normal person? What is wrong with this tool bag?"

I close my eyes and try to calm myself. "He's very sentimental."

"Okay, smashed the inside joke flowers. Got it."

Jenn studies me, waiting. After drinking some water, I find the energy to say the words out loud.

"It wasn't enough. The makeover, the dates, the jealousy, even dirty texts. It wasn't enough, Jenn. I'll always be the awkward little kid down the street."

"But I saw him when he picked you up. He looked like he wanted to eat you and not in a cannibalistic way."

I shake my head. "I think he was trying to convince himself. When it came time to actually have intercourse with me, he said he couldn't." New tears work their way out of the ducts I thought were surely unable to produce any more. "He said it was a mistake, we were a mistake."

Jenn grits her teeth. "Asshole." She glances around me.

I choke in a sob, and Jenn puts her hand on my knee. "All right, I'll get all this cleaned up. Don't worry about it. Right now, what do you want to do, Sand?"

"Sleep. I want to sleep." I lay down on the couch as I say the words. Jenn doesn't respond; she simply starts turning off all the lights. I think I feel a blanket over me, but I am unsure. My mind happily surrenders to my body's exhaustion.

The chime of the email shocks me. It's been four days since Jonny fled from me. I haven't texted him because I don't know what to say. I don't know what I want to say. He hasn't messaged me at all, not even to see if I am all right.

I am not all right.

I suppose he knows that.

I can hardly read the words on the screen because of the vibration in my hands.

Sandy-

Huge news!

Dad and I finally found a franchisee in Canada. He wants to open three stores. Finally, we're going international!!! I'll be in Canada for a couple months getting the brand off the ground here. Dad's entrusting the whole expansion to me. It's amazing.

Write me and let me know how school goes when it starts. And what second year is like. Tell me some of your nerdy medicine jokes.

Tell me you're okay.

Still your best friend,

Always,

Jonny

I throw my phone across the room.

———————————

"Canada, eh?" Lee jokes.

I hiccup into my margarita at our small dining table. "That's c-c-correct. The idea of a sexual relationship with me was so disturbing, he lllliterally fled the country."

"Yeah, well, he'll freeze his nuts off up there, so that'll be painful," Avery chimes in on the screen.

I frown. "It's July."

"But *winter is coming*," Lee whispers.

Jenn moves in front of me so they can see her on their end of the FaceTime. "Yeah and forget just his nuts. I hope he catches pneumonia and straight up dies."

Lee claps. "Oooo, dark Jenn, I like it!"

"This issssss it, you guys." I pound my drink down onto the table. Jenn removes the drink from my hand and replaces it with a glass of water. "I mean it. I took the mail app off of my phone, I blocked his phone number, and after tonight, none of us will ever speak of him again."

Lee raises her glass. "Gladly."

"It is written!" Avery yells.

Jenn laughs. "You guys are seriously the biggest lightweights I've ever seen."

"Jennifer! Affirm your agreement t-t-t-to my sweeping decllll-laration. Jonny Canton is dead."

"Jonny Canton is dead!" they all say in unison as I raise my water. They laugh and clap and cheer. I can't do any of those things. My heart hurts in my chest, and how it continues to pump anyway, I'll never understand. But I'm a scientist. Science teaches mind over matter! Science claims new neural pathways!

And just in case science fails me, I pray to God for some strength.

Strength to never think of, long for, or most importantly come in contact with my former best friend, ever again.

I love the Lord, but it's science that saves me. Not because of my mental toughness, but rather my studies. Of science. Everyone warns med students that the first year is like learning how to swim. It's difficult and exhausting.

The second year, you drown.

Everyone was correct. I am drowning. Actually, a more accurate analogy would be water torture, because as my professor claimed on our first day, we needed to be prepare to drink from a fire hose. None of us are drinking, but all of us are suffocating.

Jenn and I set alarms to remember to eat. We tell each other when our nose registers it's time to for one of us to shower. If one of us falls asleep studying, the other takes that as a cue to go to bed. It's a delicate system, but it is the only system we can manage at this time.

I'm so exhausted when I walk into the corner coffee shop, I am not sure my eyes are open. I've memorized the way, I could be moving utilizing muscle memory alone. In my head, I am reciting mnemonic devices, so I don't hear my name being called.

Thus, I am surprised when I walk into another human being as if they are a wall. A tall, hard, clean-smelling wall. I look up.

"Hey, Gorgeous," the wall rumbles.

I am suddenly very awake.

"It's only been a few weeks, Sandra. You'll adjust." Wade has a chuckle in his voice as he studies me from across the table.

"Unlikely," I reply, squirming in my seat. I am regretting my decision to skip a shower this morning. Wade laughs at my doubtful expression. "What about you? Have you adjusted to residency yet?"

"I think so, yes. It's only been a few months, but I am sure there is at least one thing I'm lacking." He takes a sip of his coffee. I frown at him. What could he possibly lack? He's perfect. "A social life."

"Ah." I nod. "I have heard of those. I think they're available to us after we finish our residencies?"

Wade chuckles. "Right." He clears his throat. "I have the apartment to myself now since the guys got matched, and at first I thought it would be so nice, having a quiet place to crash or study."

"And?"

He shrugs. "It's too quiet. Too lonely."

I lean in to clarify what he means. "Aren't you with people constantly, never home, really long shifts, working non-stop?"

He considers this. "You're right. It's not that I miss people, actually." He leans in to match my posture. "I just miss you."

My mouth drops open in surprise as my pulse picks up. My heart aches, even as it beats thunderously. Wade's warm brown eyes watch my mouth as the edges tighten into a smile. He takes this as an invitation to place his hand on mine on the table. His long fingers are cold—it is freezing in here, of course—and his touch is like a whisper. I am happy to discover I am not overwhelmed. I don't pull away.

"I know you're swamped, and I am, too, but let me be your food delivery service? My apartment can be your study room or your nap pod, I'll be your private tutor, and we can try to make it work. I think we can figure out a system, don't you?"

He squeezes my hand and knocks his knee into mine under the small table.

"We are pretty smart," I say into my coffee cup.

"You're the smart one, Gorgeous. I'll just try and keep up." He smiles and stands, extending a hand to me. I accept, letting him pull me up into a hug. He is so handsome and sweet and smart and clear about what he wants. His arms feel like a safe harbor from the storm that was med school and...everything else.

He pulls back to shine hope and desire down on me like the sun. I look up at him gladly, soaking it all up like a plant that's been stuck in the shade. He kisses my forehead, then my nose, and then my mouth. One, two, three.

CHAPTER 23

Wade and I quickly find a system that is almost exactly as he described it. He brings me meals, I study at his place, he quizzes me over coffee, and I join him for portions of his runs, as I cannot handle the distances he can. I meet with him when and where his schedule allows. We text every day and call each other most nights. We mostly talk about medicine, or we just enjoy each other's presence without talking. His schedule is hectic, but we find a happy rhythm.

A slow one.

He is gentle and patient with me when it comes to intimacy. Sometimes I would even describe him as reverent. One night I finally manage to tell him, in an uncharacteristic outburst, that I won't break and he need not be so gentle.

He loves this outburst.

Still, he is deliberate and careful. He is also exhausted. We sometimes see each other without even making out. I decide this is perfectly acceptable, because I, too, am exhausted. I am also not even remotely close to ready to attempt actual intercourse again. Wade explores me with his hands and his mouth, and I reciprocate, but I never get completely naked with him. He doesn't push me.

By mid-November, I am all but living at Wade's apartment. It's easier for us to see each other if I use his place as a home base. Plus, his apartment is lovely. It's new and sparsely decorated, and Wade keeps it tidy. Some may even call him particular, about his things and his environment, but I adapt to his preferences easily.

We are sleep together most nights. There have been a couple mornings where I think sleeping together without having sexual intercourse may be too frustrating for him. Ever in control, he simply coughs out a good morning and excuses himself to the restroom.

When we return back to Wade's place after seeing our respective families for Thanksgiving, Wade is energized. He has two days off in a row, and he spends them with me, in bed. He doesn't push me, but he does, finally, ask.

"Sandra." He grips me where his hand is on my hip. We're lying in his bed facing each other. "I'm in no hurry, here. If you want to wait until marriage, if you're still a virgin, I don't care what it is, Gorgeous. I just feel like you're not letting me in. Will you tell me why you won't let me see you naked? Why we can do everything but intercourse?"

I sit up. "All right."

In a long conversation that requires all of my mental and emotional strength, I tell Wade about Jonny. I summarize the unrequited crush from ages twelve to twenty, but I provide more details regarding our recent history. Wade grows quiet at times. He stands, he curses, he paces.

"You're angry," I say, watching him carve a path in the rug by his bed.

He stops walking and exhales. "Yes, Sandra, I'm a little pissed!"

I nod. "At me."

He looks at me, and his frown softens by a small fraction. "Not really. Well, yes, that you said he was just your friend when clearly he wasn't. I would've asked then, made sure you were really ready to go on a double date with them. And for the record," he steps toward me and raises his voice louder than I've ever heard him before, "I didn't kiss you good night, or move faster with you, because you were skittish as hell, Sandra! You were so nervous and tense, that night especially, and I didn't want to scare you off!"

He resumes pacing. "I'm pissed at him for getting into your head so badly, and most of all I'm pissed at myself. For being scared of how I was already falling in love with you. I mean, we only had a couple months to go. I should've convinced you. Forget the damn rules or rumors and fuck my stupid residency. I never should have let you go!"

His words ring out in the apartment like a gong. We are both panting as if we've just finished a cardiovascular workout. Wade sighs, relaxing first between the two of us.

"I'm sorry. I shouldn't have raised my voice like that." He looks up at me, and it takes me a minute to recognize the look on his face. Hurt. I ache in my chest again, knowing he looks like that because of me. He steps up to the bed where I'm sitting. "I need to know, is it finished with him? Is it over?"

"Yes, Wade. I blocked his number. I haven't spoken to him since that night in July."

He climbs onto the bed and sits in front of me. He reaches out a hand to touch my knee but stops. His voice cracks when he looks up at me. "And if he comes back tomorrow and tries to win you back?"

"It wouldn't matter." I reach out and touch him first, putting a hand on his shoulder. "And he won't, anyway. He doesn't think of me like that, as a woman."

Wade scoffs. "Then he's an idiot. A blind idiot. I'm still mad and hurt, and yet all I want to do is rip that thin tank top right off of you."

I laugh and climb up to straddle him. He shudders.

"Well, then, why don't you?"

He smiles and rests his forehead on mine. "You're so brilliant Dr. Sandra Hayes. And sexy. And I love you."

"I lllllove you, too." I kiss Wade as soon as I get the words out. I do love him. He's perfect for me in every way. We're perfect together. But at saying the words out loud, my chest explodes with heat and pain, in a way I can't fully process. I rub my hand on my sternum to alleviate some of the pressure. It doesn't help.

Wade moans into my mouth, and I focus on driving him crazy. If I disrupt his one-two-three pattern, his brain misfires. I love it. He makes a move to push me onto my back, but I push him down instead. I hover over my sweet, tall, dark, handsome doctor. He's beautiful. And there is still hurt in his eyes. I begin to slip off his boxers and show him just how much he means to me.

CHAPTER 24

When Wade asked if we should spend Christmas together, with our families, the answer was obvious. He's met my parents already, and I've met his, since neither Tulsa nor Dallas is that far away. Wade's parents are warm and welcoming, as are mine, in their own way. Wade doesn't mind their idiosyncrasies. If there's anyone who can charm a scientist and a doctor, it's my future spine surgeon boyfriend.

My brothers seem to approve of him, not that their approval means too much to me, since we've never been close. Deon does seem to study us during the Christmas celebrations, as if waiting or looking for something. I don't think he ever finds it.

After spending the first couple days of our break with my family, we head to Dallas for Christmas Day and the day after. I meet Wade's sister, and while she is friendly, I don't feel that I've gotten her seal of approval. Although I am not the best at reading social cues, especially from strangers. Her most repeated commentary is about how smart she's heard I am, and how alike Wade and I are. I assume those are good things.

After a delicious Christmas feast, we exchange gifts. It is unpleasant. It's awkward to open gifts to and from people you know, but with strangers, it is unbearable. The gifts from his parents and sister are sensible, if not personal. Wade agrees to exchange gifts with me later, in private. His parents and sister make a fuss of making more homemade eggnog, providing us with our opportunity to slip upstairs.

"Let's get out of here. I don't want to give you my gift in my childhood bedroom."

I laugh. "Okay."

I grab my coat and his gift, and Wade leads me out the front door. We walk seemingly aimlessly, holding hands in comfortable silence. It's cold out, but not blistering. Wade finally slows when we reach the center of his family's very nice neighborhood. There's a greenbelt stretched before us and small manmade waterfall in front of us. We sit on an old wooden bench. The sun is setting over the rooftops of the houses, putting on a beautiful display.

"Can I open first?" Wade asks, looking excited.

"It's nothing big," I warn him. "Don't look so intrigued."

He laughs but shrugs me off. He pulls it out and smiles. It's a coffee thermos that reads, *You must be aphasia, because you leave me speechless.* I added an engraving into the stainless steel that reads, *Love, Sandra.*

"I love it," he chuckles. Then he pulls out a small box about the same size as the one I gave him. I wonder if he got me a coffee mug. Inside the box is another box, and inside that, a small velvet box.

Is this...

I begin to tremble so badly I drop the box off the bench and down to the ground before I can even open it. I yelp.

"Let me," Wade calms me, adding, "I wanted to get down here anyway."

He's on one knee.

Wade is down on one knee!

"Dr. Sandra Hayes...Gorgeous. You are the most brilliant woman I've ever met. I can't get enough of that mind of yours. I know our schedules are crazy and our futures are unclear, but I'm clear on one thing. I won't ask you to take my last name, but I will ask you to take my hand. I love you so much, Sandra. Will you marry me?"

Wade Anderson just asked me to marry him.

He's so beautiful and his eyes are searching mine like they hold the key to explaining dark matter.

"Yes!" I cry, literally, as a shocked tear falls from my right eye. My chest seizes with the familiar ache I can't seem to alleviate. I apply pressure to the sensation with my right hand while Wade grabs my left. He slips on the platinum ring that supports a huge, beautiful solitary diamond. *The ring must have cost a fortune,* I think to myself as Wade wraps his arms around me.

He says something about lucky man and girl genius, but all I can hear is the blood pumping around my eardrums. Wade takes my face in his hands and kisses me one, two, three, adjust, one, two, three. With my pulse and my chest pains, I start to focus on my arms... One, two, three, adjust, one, two, three, adjust... Do I have arm pain?

Am I having a heart attack?!

"I would say an abnml crdiac rthrm is expetd," Lee swallows, "during a surprise proposal."

"Lee, the crunching! It's the day after Christmas. Why aren't you eating turkey leftovers?"

She scoffs. "Lucky Charms is superior to turkey in every single way."

"Protein content?"

"But back to you."

"Yeah." I lower my voice again as I listen to confirm Wade is still in the shower. "This is a normal physical response to such large stimuli?"

"This is? Wait, you're not still having chest pains?"

I take a deep breath and focus on my pulse, my chest, my systems in general. I feel the urge to rub my heart, even though the pressure is gone. "No, I'm not."

"K. Then I hold my position that yes, that reaction was normal. What did your parents say?"

I nod. "They said happy words with their mouths, but their facial expressions conveyed what you'd guess: that I should focus on med school."

"Expected and understandable reaction. And his parents, the teacher, and the pediatrician, right?"

"Right. They seem genuinely thrilled. Apparently Wade has told them all about me since I enrolled in his class last spring."

I hear a dramatic sigh before I hear her voice. "Yes, yes, the prodigy. Why wouldn't he drone on?" Her face reappears with a smile. "And is his sister so easily impressed, and what did your brothers say?"

"No, and nothing. Our siblings don't appear to be cheering us on."

"Eh, they are on the outside of your combined brilliance looking in, mere civilians."

"Lee," I scold. "How many times must we review this? Doctors are not part of the armed forces."

"I know, but we also serve humanity with our lives! Now! Show me the ring again!"

I do, and I can't help but smile at her exclamations. A text comes through. I explain to Lee what I'm looking at on my screen. "Jenn says it's so hot that he didn't ask me to take his last name."

"Getting it now." Lee's focus shifts to our group thread. "Avery disagrees. She wants a man who wants to *brand her with his own surname*? I think I just threw up my rainbow marshmallows."

We both laugh. I hear Wade turn the shower off, so I tell Lee I need to hang up. As I end the call, I feel significantly better.

CHAPTER 25

JON

"Yeah, well, look at the daggum sign, stupid!" I yell at my windshield. *Shit, they probably recognize me or my truck.* I make the international sign of driver surrender that explains *I'm* the idiot.

And I am.

The world's largest moron.

Numbnuts Supreme, as Rob has always said.

For kissing my best friend.

For touching her, tasting her, and then breaking her heart. Staring up at me like she was twelve all over again.

I ruined everything.

Fourteen years down the drain in less than seven days.

Classic Captain Dipshit. *Ugh!*

"Move!" I scream at the New Year's Eve traffic. The screaming and waving doesn't make us move faster or make me feel any better. I'm just desperate to get there, desperate to see her. Will she even be there? I wouldn't expect her at anything associated with my family after what I did, but I'm supposed to be in Canada right now, so maybe she will. Plus, it's tradition. I know her parents will be there, and they'll want her there, too.

Please be there.

After an eternity of honking my horn and yelling into the abyss, I pull into the country club's parking lot. I toss my keys to the valet and rush through the big gaudy doors. Once I hit the ballroom doors, I scan the crowd as quickly as I can. I have to talk to her, get her to listen to me. She hasn't texted me back in months. She hasn't responded weekly or even sent an emoji reaction, and I seriously feel like I'm dying. We have to go back to how we were. I know she misses me, too; she has to. *Where is she? Where is she? Where is she?*

"Jon?"

Sandy. But she called me Jon? What the— She's here with him. My whole body pulls tight like a resistance band.

And she is *not* happy to see me. "I thought yyyyou were in C-c-c-canada."

I grit my teeth. "Well, Sand, maybe if you read my one thousand messages—"

"She changed her number, asshole." The pretty doctor dares to speak to me. The prick who doesn't kiss my girl good night is glaring at me.

Not that I want him kissing her.

I glare right back. "Uh, I'm sorry, you've known her, what, fifteen minutes? Sit down, buddy, the grownups are talking right now."

"You—"

I don't hear what Wade says as he actually takes a swing at me, clearly having never thrown a punch in his life. I evade his hit and tackle him at the waist. He tries to fight me, but it's pretty laughable.

"You're fit, but let me guess, you're a runner." I grunt. We crash to the ground, but I pop right back up to spit a threat at him. "Stay down and keep your million-dollar fingers intact, Doc."

"J-J-Jonny!"

There she is.

Pissed and stammering at me.

Damn, she's so pretty. I wonder if I tackled *her* and ran with her over my shoulder until we're alone if I could kiss her again. Watch her crazy beautiful mind shut off underneath me. *No! Focus, Jonny!*

I focus.

And I see it, on her hand as she reaches down to comfort the tall, dark pansy-ass.

A ring.

A ring?!

"You're *engaged* to this guy? Oh, wow, okay. Well, that's just perfect. Just great."

Someone is grabbing me by the arms and pulling me from her. "C'mon, son, that's enough."

I just look at her. Only her. "Tell me, Sandy, does he still make you stutter?"

"Jon, seriously? Shut up!" My brother is yanking at my shoulder, but I shrug free.

She's still looking at me. "No, forget that. Does he make you stop, Sandy? Does he make your brain shut off? Does he? *Does he*?"

Three men have their hands on me. I shrug and pull, but the doors to the ballroom slam shut in my face.

Sandy's Dad steps into view. "You need to let her go, son. It's time to let her go."

"But I—"

"You're done here, Jon." My dad joins Sandy between me and the doors. "You've made a scene and embarrassed the Canton name at our own damn party. Get out of here. Now!"

I growl in frustration and, just to piss him off, yell every expletive I can think of on my way out of the lobby. I don't care about the Canton name. I don't care what the whole town thinks.

She.

Can't.

Marry.

Him.

SANDRA

"I'm all right. I'm fine." Wade shrugs me off, clearly embarrassed about the altercation. I am unsure of what to do or say. Hundreds of people are staring in our direction. The oldies holiday music has stopped. Wade is panting. Jonny is screaming obscenities in the lobby.

"Well! I was not expecting that at a neighborhood party in Tulsa, Oklahoma! Y'all really know how to throw down!" Jenn proclaims the statement to the whole room. People laugh and music resumes. I let out a breath it appears I was holding in.

Jenn grabs my hand. "Sand, want to go to the ladies' room for a minute?"

I am unable to nod.

Wade looks down at me, eyes wide and hands still shaking. "Are you all right, Sandra?"

Jenn starts to lead me away. "She will be. I'm just going to go remind her how to breathe, and we'll be right back."

In the women's bathroom, Jenn sets me down on a small padded stool, and I feel my entire self dissolve. Jonny's angry face and Wade's shock play in my mind over and over, like a show that gets caught buffering. I want to turn the show off, but I can't. *"Does he make your brain shut off? Does he? Does he?"*

"Hey, look at me. It's over." Jenn squats down into my line of sight. "Everyone out there already moved on to talk about the crab cakes."

"Unlllllikely."

Jenn laughs. "Yeah, that was a lie. That was the craziest thing I've ever seen in person! Everyone will be talking about it for weeks." I groan, and she recovers her train of thought. "Sorry! Not weeks. But it doesn't matter anyway because this isn't your life anymore, Sand. I love that you had me come meet your parents, and it was nice of you and Wade to join in a holiday tradition, but this is all your past. Who cares about these people?"

I bite my lip and close my eyes. As I do, the images flash through my mind again. Jonny's face losing all its color when Wade said I'd changed my number. Wade assaulting him, only to be tackled to the floor in less than a second. All the people looking on.

"Sandra. Jonny, do you want to talk about it?"

My eyes open at the mention of his name. I open my mouth to speak but can't pinpoint what to say. I don't know what I feel, other than the irritating pressure around my heart as it pumps.

"Well, *I'll* talk about it. I think he's a piece of shit. Coming back here now, after you're engaged and happy, because he wants you back in his life. From what you told me, it's always been what he wants. Jonny wants you as a friend. Jonny wants you as a cheerleader. Jonny wants you as a girlfriend, then suddenly doesn't. Jonny can screw off and die. He doesn't get a say anymore. This is your life, and you do what you want." I try to nod. Jenny leans back. "Maybe the question is what *do* you want?"

"I want to go home."

I barely have the sentence out before she's standing and pulling me up. She wipes my tears and straightens my sparkly top before leading me out of the door where Wade is waiting just outside. She tells him it's time to go, and soon we're in the car driving all the way back to the city, which was not our original plan.

Wade holds my hand but doesn't talk. Jenn occasionally says something from the backseat. The two of them handle grabbing our bags and loading the car. I'm sure the air in the car is tense and thick, but I can barely breathe it. I am overloaded. Even Wade's soft stroking of my hand with his thumb is too stimulating. I don't pull away; I just sit. Somewhere after we leave the Tulsa city limits, I fall asleep.

CHAPTER 26

"**Y**ou look stunning."

"Totally banging. Wade's crazy system of smoothies and protein bars really filled you back out."

Jenn joins in with Lee and Avery. "Yassss! Peak Sandra! I'm glad we didn't take it in again. You got a little skeletal there for a while. Now you're really glowing."

My mother sniffs. "You are. You look so happy!"

Lee groans. "Dr. Hayes, please, no more crying! You'll get her going and your daughter will wake up with extra fluids around her eyes and nose and walk down the aisle looking like a Tetraodontidae."

"A what?"

"Puffer fish," Avery and I answer Jenn in unison.

My mother laughs at us. "I'm sorry. I'm just so happy you're happy, Sandra."

I am. I look at my reflection, somewhat amazed. My slim white dress fits appropriately now, and the beading on the halter top casts sparkles around my face. Jenn has perfectly styled my dark gold waves for the rehearsal dinner and mastered my preference for minimal makeup. I look at my girlfriends in the mirror.

We're all a bit, well, I think the right word would be giddy, having just aced our last test of the year.

I am happy. My life is perfect except for the nagging twists inside my chest cavity. My general physician assured me it's just the stress of finishing my second year of med school and planning a wedding in five months, even a small and sensible wedding.

I didn't correct her that Wade had actually done most of the planning. He'd made a spreadsheet and a calendar and kept us on track. My parents felt the process was rushed, but Wade made solid, logical arguments. We had already decided to marry. He had a few vacation days he could schedule to use right after I finished my exams. There was no reason to delay. My hand goes to my chest without my knowledge.

"Quit doing that! This is why acne keeps appearing in your cleavage!" Lee scolds.

Avery bumps her at the hip. "He won't care about that, believe me." She lowers her voice to a loud whisper. "But I do wonder if when you finally do it, it'll be one, two, three, pause, one, two, three, doneski!"

"Avery!" I screech, looking to make sure my mother has made it all the way out of the room. My friends laugh heartily. "Ugh, I never should have told you about that. He's not that way all the time." They all three share in a look at each other and then at me and then laugh again, revealing that they do not believe my claim. Eventually, I laugh, too, as I have wondered internally myself what Avery was bold enough to say out loud. I suppose tomorrow night I'll finally find out.

I rub my chest again.

The girls help me get out of my gown and into my rehearsal dinner dress. We head to the restaurant and enjoy a beautiful evening. Wade is gentle and attentive, as always. The small affair is quiet but cheery. Our parents and siblings give short toasts, seemingly happy for us, finally. Wade drops me off at Jenn's apartment that I used to share.

"Tell me you love me, Gorgeous," Wade whispers at the door. He is relaxed and smiling wide, but the musculature around his eyes is tight. He has asked me this over and over since New Year's Eve. Every time I smile and assure him I love him before kissing him hard and fast. He always slows us down with a careful touch. He tells me he'll see me at the altar and then kisses me good night. One, two, three.

The girls all but attack me when I make it into the apartment. They gush about the evening and the details of the schedule in the morning. I nod along while using a considerable amount of my mental energy to calm my pulse and keep my hand off of my chest. When we begin our bedtime rotations in and out of the shared bathroom, my phone buzzes. I smile, knowing Wade always messages me good night. But the text is from an unknown number.

You're short a Best Man, Sandy. Please, please check your email. Our email.

Jonny.

I fall back against the living room wall and slide to the floor. The few bites of pasta I managed to eat earlier threaten an evacuation. I close my eyes and breathe. I haven't heard from him since the altercation on New Year's Eve months ago. Now he contacts me? On the night before my wedding? My wedding! I'm getting married!

I'm happy, focused, and have all the things I always wanted.

And he messages me now.

Now, here I am, my legs itching from contact dermatitis from the dust on the engineered wood floor.

I should not be shocked. I should have expected this. It would have been prudent to change my phone number. I knew, years ago, my love for Jonny would somehow ruin my life. I was proven correct.

I just did not expect this, here, now on the eve of my wedding. *My wedding!*

I remember Jenn's words from the last time we spoke of him. I've barely let myself think of him since then. My mental toughness has improved considerably. Because she was right.

It is always what Jonny wants, when he wants it, and how. He said Best Man—does this mean he's ready to be my friend again? To come to the wedding and support me, feel happy for me, as he should have done all along? Does he want to try to change my mind? Does he want—

No, synapses! No! What do I want? What do I want?

I want to read the email. Perhaps I should be strong enough not to. Maybe I am a bad fiancé or a weak woman. So be it. I am and have always been deeply curious. I can't not know.

I open a new browser window on my phone and type in the account and password information I could never forget even if I wanted to. I drop the phone out of shaking hands when I see the number in the circle. There are sixty-five unread emails.

I squeeze my eyes shut. Sixty-five! I don't hear the girls talking in the next room; I don't smell the soap; I don't feel the floor underneath me. Too much stimuli. My brain cannot...my chest... *shit!*

Breathe, Sandra. Breathe, lungs!

A few minutes pass before I pick the phone up from my lap. I squint to focus my vision at the top of the screen where I see in all caps, "JUST READ THIS ONE." My vision clears, and I recognize the smell of Jenn's overnight body serum. My body is recovering. So I tap on the letters.

Sandy,

There is a lot of text below but just start with these first few sentences, one paragraph at a time, if you decide you want to keep reading. I really hope you do.

I realize now that you didn't change your number; you just blocked mine. I understand your decision. But if I'd known, I would've gotten a new number months ago. Not to make you respond, or force our friendship—as hard as it would be for me not to!—but to ask you to check these emails.

I wrote a couple updates from Canada, but they were shit. Don't bother with those. It's the ones that start on New Year's Eve that are important. But I just found out the wedding is tomorrow... I just wrote a few choice words about how I feel about that but deleted them. Please acknowledge this as a sign of personal growth on my part!!!

Now I'm short on time, so I copied and pasted the most important ones in this email. Just scroll down.
Jonny

Dear Sandy,

I need you to know I didn't leave because I didn't want to make love to you or because I'm not in love with you. I left because I'm a moron and a coward. When you looked up at me, just before I had my nervous break-down, your eyes looked exactly like they had as kids. Looking at me like I'm some kind of superhero. Like I'm perfect. I'm not!

I remember one time, ONE time in our teens, you turned to me and said, "Sometimes, Jonny, you're quite obtuse." I think that was the only time you had me pegged. Shit, Sandy, I brought you home to my house with pictures of Layla all over the place! I didn't even notice, didn't even think.

Then after I left, I really spiraled—which is what I de-served for leaving you like that. I'm so sorry. I pray every day that somehow you'll forgive me, that you'll write me back, text me back. But you haven't.

And I understand it, because as I was saying, my spiral-ing—I didn't see you, Sandy. You were there all along, and I didn't see you fully. How can I deserve you now? I don't. I never will.

Now my only hope is that somehow I can earn back your friendship.

Because these months without you have been the worst of my life.
I absolutely cannot live without you.
So I'll keep writing.
Jonny

Wait, I need to clarify something from my last email. You were always a beautiful girl. I remember I told you you were "kinda adorable" the first time you snort-laughed when you were nine. I always thought you were cute as a button. Even when we got a little older, I could see you were pretty. I was just so distracted by...my own issues, I didn't pay attention to much else.
At the opera that night, Rob said you were too good for me, then you looked up at me like I was the damn sun and all I could think was, Rob's right, Rob's right, Rob's right.
I was scared shitless I'd never be able to rise to your standards of, well, absolute perfection. Perfect grades, perfect choices, perfect everything.
So I left.
I'm so sorry I did.
Love,
Jonny

Jenn startles when she sees me. "Sand? What are you doing on the floor? Are you okay?"

I manage to hold out a hand, not looking away from my phone. I hear Lee say something about dragons and necessary escapism. Avery assures Jenn I can be left alone for a while, but Jenn sets a glass of water down beside me before leaving the room. At least I think that's what it is. I haven't looked up. All I can do is keep reading.

Sandra,
Sounds wrong, doesn't it?
I hate that you called me Jon.
I hate that you're with someone who probably deserves you. Someone who is perfect for you. Someone who IS perfect, just like you are.
I hate that I don't know how your tests are going, what all your clinical stuff is like that you were so looking forward to.
I hate that you're living out all the things you always wanted, but without me.
I hate myself for letting that happen.
Jonny

In my defense, you had never dressed sexy a day in our lives! You hid all your perfect curves under friggin' boy clothes! I mean, give a guy a break!

Hey, Sand. Sorry for that last email. Sometimes I get really pissed.

I'm trying to decide what a good man would do. I keep praying about it, but the good book doesn't have an explicit example for me.

Would a good man step aside and let you marry Doctor Perfect? Someone who can understand your job, talk science with you, stick with systems, and keep their clutter in drawers and their clothes neatly folded?

OR!

Would a good man stop you from settling for the safe, easy choice that will never push you, never overwhelm you, never excite you, never make you snort-laugh? (I'm assuming he never has. If he has, just let me believe this lie. I beg you.)

I think the better man would do the latter, even if it's harder on everyone involved, including me. Is that stupid?

Your Jonny

Sandy,

Sometimes when I'm working out, blood pumping and adrenaline flowing, I just let all my anger out. And all I can see is that asshole's mouth on your neck at dinner. Something snapped in me, like a dam breaking—how had I never had my lips on your neck? How had I never held you, tasted you? How could I know your heart and brain like my own and not your body?

The worst part of it, though, the part that gets me doing rep after rep until my muscles shake, is how you looked up at him, the way you used to look at me.

I am such a gigantic idiot. Have I mentioned that?
I'm sorry it took seeing another man's hands on you to realize the only kind of man I want to be is yours.
Love,
Jonny

S-

I was looking back through my emails feeling pathetic, and I wanted to make it explicitly clear, because sometimes, Sweetheart, you need non-science stuff clearly spelled out:
I very, very much want to have sex with you.
I am, without a doubt, completely in love with you. I think part of me always has been. I know part of me always will be.
-J

Sandy,

In middle school you went through that weird obsession with babies and birth and families and stuff. I'm pretty sure, looking back, you got your first lady time of the month and were coping by memorizing everything about the reproductive systems.
Anyway, you said you wanted to grow up and get married to a trophy husband, become a surgeon, have two boys and a dog and even a minivan. You said you'd schedule your surgeries around little league football.

That sounds so absolutely perfect.

You know I have the muscles to be your token husband.

In fact, I bet when you said that back then you meant me, didn't you?

I hope you did.

I know I don't deserve it.

I know I messed up.

But I hope you still want all of that. I do.

I want it all with you.

Jonny

Sandy,

I am really starting to freak the hell out now, that you'll never talk to me ever again. I thought the sex email would do it. Or the trophy husband one. I sat and thought and thought and thought (probably pulled something!) and realized maybe I didn't do a good enough job of apologizing.

I'm so sorry I hurt you.

I'm sorry I left you in such a vulnerable moment.

I'm sorry I wasted so many years not with you, as your boyfriend.

I'm sorry I took you for granted for our whole lives.

I'm sorry I can be a distracted, narcissistic asshole.

I'm sorry I didn't tell you every day that you're my favorite person and the tornado that day all those years ago was the best thing that ever happened to me. (That little

twister didn't touch down long enough to kill or injure
anyone so I think it's okay for me to say that.)
I'm sorry I complicated everything between us.
I'm sorry I wasn't a good friend, giving you space to date
and get over me.
I'm sorry I chickened out when you needed me most.
I'm sorry I tackled your fiancé.
Please forgive me,
Love,
Jonny
PS: We both know the last one is a lie.

I'd like to discuss the roles and responsibilities of a Tro-
phy Husband, but I can't, because you're still not talking
to me. Going from reading your words every week for
fourteen years, to seeing them daily, to hearing your
voice and seeing you laugh all the time to this, this radio
silence. I'm wrecked. I guess I've been forgetting to eat.
Thad says I've lost a ton of muscle mass. Rob says I'm
missing things at work. I don't care.
I do care about how I can support you, what that would
look like. I think if I know your schedule, I can plan my
trips for when you have tests coming up, and you'll want
your space. I looked into a meal delivery service, be-
cause you can't cook for shit. I can grill dinner for you,
but you need lunches and meals for when I'm traveling.
You can't survive on just sugary coffee and Cheetos.
I already have Maryann for all your laundry.

Obviously I will get ripped and stay in top Trophy shape for you. I'll give you neck massages and carry you to bed when you fall asleep on your books. But also please tell me a big part of a Trophy Husband is sex because I am all for being your sex slave.

Whatever you need to become the brilliant surgeon you are destined to be.

And what you don't need, too, silly stuff, to keep you laughing and turn your brain off.

All of it.

Sign me up.

Jonny

Enough of this, Sandy, because if we take a step back here and think logically, look at the data available, we can both agree this is all YOUR FAULT!

I suck in what is possibly the deepest breath I've ever breathed. My fault? *My fault!?*

In a fit of rage, I open my text messages.

> **Me: Logically conclude this is MY FAULT!?**
> **Me: WTF!**
> 1(555)989-2453: Yes, come downstairs and discuss this with me. You need to see reason, Doc.

I push myself up and turn to face the living room window that overlooks the street. Jonny's truck is sitting right outside our building. My body begins to move so quickly my consciousness doesn't even realize what's happening.

That I am almost running to the very thing I've tried to avoid for almost a year.

CHAPTER 27

"**F**inally! I thought you were supposed to be some kind of speed reader?" Jonny exhales, sounding relieved, as soon as I walk outside.

I freeze and do the only thing I'm capable of doing in this moment, which is growling in frustration.

"Get in the truck, Sandy." Jonny opens the door for me. "I'm not taking you anywhere. I just don't think we should yell at each other in the street."

"Fine!" I do yell the word, surprising myself. I jump when my door slams. I try to focus my thoughts as I watch Jonny walk around the front and get in. He glares at me, which irks me further because he has no right to be doing any such glaring. I get to glare!

"So, Doc, are you ready to discuss this rationally?"

My jaw is clenched tight. "You are a b-b-b-"

"Bastard, I know."

"Don't do that!"

Jonny deflates in his seat. "Okay, I'm sorry."

Deep breath. "Jonny. How could this possibly be my ffffault?"

He grins one of his angry smiles. "Because you never spoke up, Sandy."

"What?"

He raises his brows at me. "Did you? Did you ever come clean about how you felt? Did you ever flirt or try to kiss me or *anything* in thirteen damn years?"

"You knew how I felt about you!" I shout the words.

"Maybe when you were twelve! That you had a little crush on me! You grew out of it! Or I thought you did. I had no clue you ever thought about me as anything other than a third brother."

"Imp-p-possible."

He shifts in his seat to face me fully. "Is it, Sandy? Have you ever spoken up for yourself, *with words,* ever? Did you ever tell your parents you didn't want to take so many classes? Did you ever tell Deon to quit calling you squirt when you hated it your whole life? I bet Wade runs your whole damn life, and it kills me! I bet he planned your wedding. I bet he schedules your laundry and other shit I can't bear to even think about, doesn't he? Have you ever said any of the big, scary, honest stuff out loud?"

Again my mouth falls open, but I can't make sound come out. It's fairly predictable that I would let Wade take charge in my life, but how could Jonny know he planned the wedding? And our laundry system? Do I even want a laundry system? Do I really never speak up for myself?

The sound of our breathing is loud around us until Jonny speaks up again, his voice much softer. "You're so busy trying to be perfect for everyone, and for yourself, and then what? So you have perfect scores and pass boards and never mess up a surgery and have quiet robot sex every Tuesday night and then

you'll be happy? Then you'll have finally made it to some destination your parents set for you?"

"Oh, and you know how to live life so well? C-c-cowering in
the shadows of your big brother so no one expects anything of
you? So you can just be Fun Jonny? So no one will call you stupid? There's nothing wrong with pushing for big g-g-goals, Jonny. You should try it sometime."

"I know!"

This is an unexpected reply. "What?"

"Shit, you're pretty when you're angry with me. Have I ever
told you that?"

"J-J-J—"

"Okay! Sand. Okay. Sorry. You're right, and I did push. I am. I
heard your voice in my head, I even re-read some of your emails
to pump myself up, and I told Dad to let me take over the Canada
expansion without him or Uncle Jim. And he agreed." He smiles
a sad smile.

My pulse becomes erratic at the thought of it, of him finally
stepping into all that he is. I'm so proud of him my voice cracks.
"That's awesome, Jonny."

His big teal eyes look away with a tight chuckle. "It's also
irrelevant right now." He takes a deep breath. "We need some
conclusions here, Brainiac. I know of at least two big questions
we need to answer." He looks back at me, and I can't read all of
the emotions on his face. There are too many. "First one, do you
think you can forgive me?"

I don't know what to say. Can I? Should I? Will I?

"Sandy, sweetheart, I'm so sorry for hurting you. I never
should've left your apartment. I should've stayed and talked it

out. I should've come back the next morning and groveled. I will never hurt you like that again, I promise you. I'm so, so sorry," He reaches out and grabs my hand, collapsing it into his and squeezing. "Sandy? Say something."

"I don't know," I whisper. I remember vividly how exposed I was, cold and bare underneath him, and he just left. I also keep re-reading the words of his emails in my mind. *Sorry* and *trophy husband* and *in love with me.*

"Okay." It comes out garbled. Jonny clears his throat. "Okay. Let's progress to question two for now. Do you still love me?"

In this moment, as tears fill my eyes and a sensation of relief fills my chest cavity, I know my fate. I will never not love Jonny Canton. It's not logical or rational. He has hurt me more than anyone my entire life.

He isn't wrong about our past, however. I wasn't clear about what I wanted. I hid behind my grades and my plans and never took any real risks. I look at him now; his eyes are brimming with tears. He is also hurting. Badly.

In fact, he looks terrible.

"Are you sick?" I blurt.

"Thinking about it! Based on the answer to my question, I can't remember what I was able to eat today, but I think we're fixin' to find out." He grabs the bridge of his nose with a shaking hand.

"You know I'll always llllove you, Jonny."

He shakes his head. "But are you still in love with me? Do you still think about me? Almost all day long? Do you relive our first kiss on July Fourth over and over?" His voice lowers an octave. "Or that night right here in that seat of this truck?"

I do. All of those things. My answer comes out as a sob. "Every d-d-d-"

"Oh, thank God!" He takes both of my hands in his. "Don't cry, sweetheart. I'm here now. We're together. We'll fix this."

I pull my hands out of his and hold them to my head. I shake it slowly and squeeze my eyes shut, trying to grasp onto coherent thoughts. "Jonny, I'm getting married tomorrow."

"The fuck you are!" I open my eyes to find his eyes bulging from his face as his voice raises. "The only way you're going down the aisle tomorrow is if I can get Pastor Tim up here in time and a new marriage license from the clerk. I don't think they'll give us a license on a Saturday."

I close my eyes again. I continue to shake and squeeze my cranium. I hear Jonny mutter something and leave the truck. My door opens.

"Get out of the truck, Sandy. C'mon." He motions down with his hand, but I am not sure I want to move. Before I can speak, he reaches in and pulls me out, setting me down in front of him. He puts his forehead on mine. The scent of him surrounds me. "You need to get your head straight, but I'm not going to kiss you with another man's ring on your finger. A ring that is not at all you, by the way. That thing is obscene. Anyway. What I'm gonna do is I'm gonna hold you now, tight as hell, and hope that's enough."

He holds my head tight where his chest meets his shoulder with one hand, while the other wraps around my back like a clamp. His body is hot like always, and his squeeze is not gentle. His breathing is shaky, as is my own. But the smell of him, the heat, it thrills my senses. And the stabbing sensation in my chest finally subsides.

I don't know how long we stand there. I notice when the hand around my back moves to stroke me up and down. He applies significant pressure, up and down and around, like a back rub. His hand slips low on my back, and then he stops moving it. He shakes around me and grips me tighter. But that momentary pause, the feel of his touch shifting from comfort to something else, it floods me.

I start to cry.

All my systems are overcome.

Jonny whispers that he's sorry over and over again.

I just don't want him to stop holding me.

I don't care about the wedding or my family or the dress or my phone that is exploding with messages from my three very concerned friends.

All I care about is Jonny.

Which means he's right.

No wedding tomorrow.

No honeymoon flight tomorrow night.

I'm going to have to tell Wade.

I'm going to break him.

Break everything.

Finally I pull back to look up, but Jonny doesn't give me much room.

"You ruined my life, Jonny! Now everything is ffffffalling apart!"

"I know I did, Sand, I know. But I promise you, I'll help you put it back together. We'll fix it, together, I promise."

"How do I know you won't hurt me ag-g-g—"

"Because you know I won't. I can't function without you. Look at me, I'm a mess! I look like shit!"

I'm still sobbing. "You really do."

Jonny laughs, but it sounds like he is trying not to sob himself. "I know. I know I'll have to prove it, Sand, and I will. I'll be by your side, proving myself every single second of everyday. I won't let you down again."

He clamps down around me again. I manage to stop sobbing.

I talk into his shirt. "Wade."

Jonny releases me to open the truck door. "Yup, let's go to his place right now."

"What time is it?"

"It's time to break up with Doctor Pansy-Ass. That's what the hell time it is."

"Jonny!"

He glares at me. "What, woman? You make me crazy! I could say I'm sorry, but that would be a lie! Now get in the truck, Sandy!"

"Okay!" I yell.

I climb in the seat, and the love of my life drives me to my fiancé's apartment at one a.m. on my wedding day.

KELSEY HUMPHREYS

CHAPTER 28

Jonny promised to be by my side every second, and he was. He stayed in his truck in the street while I broke up with Wade. Which was excruciating.

However, Jonny had assured me that if Wade knew me at all, he would not be blindsided. Jonny was correct. Wade was hurt and disappointed, but I saw nothing in his reaction that resembled shock. Which surprised me. It would have been truly terrible for such a wonderful man to settle for a woman who was in love with someone else. I told him so. He was not very receptive to my feedback. I also told him I hoped we could remain friends. He told me I should leave. I understood.

Jonny held my hand and kept quiet on the drive back to Jenn's apartment. He slept on the couch, knowing he would not be well-received by my friends the next morning. He did not argue with their harsh assessment of him and the entire situation.

He drove me to the hotel to tell my parents the news. They were disappointed but sympathetic when I explained I didn't love Wade. They had an altogether different reaction when I mentioned I was finally going to be with Jonny.

Jonny was smart to wait in the lobby.

He helped me gather items from the church and even from Wade's apartment during an appointed time when Wade wouldn't be home. He got us meals and typed out group texts and cancellation emails. He stopped everything every couple hours and just held me, standing around me like a human shield. Or blanket. Or home.

He took a few days off to help me make returns and to pack my things. Then he moved me home to Tulsa, back into my childhood bedroom. He kissed my head and cheeks and hands, but not my mouth. He said I needed time to recover, and he was right.

He told me at least twenty-two times that he was sorry and that he'd make it up to me. The more tired and sadder I looked, the more he'd tell me how wonderful and beautiful I was, but overall he was surprisingly quiet.

Until one week later, a week since I climbed into his truck and dismantled my life. Jonny asked if he could take me out on a date. He messaged me all day long. He was supposed to be working from home, but I don't see how he could have been getting anything else done other than searching for memes and songs to text me.

He showed up looking better than ever, even if still a little lean. He took me to dinner and, to my surprise, bowling. Of course, Jonny is a master bowler. I am not. We laughed all night, and when he dropped me off on my parents' doorstep, he kissed me in a way I can't describe, because it short circuited my brain and all of my body's functions.

We had the same evening the following night, only it was roller skating instead of bowling. Jonny canceled multiple work trips so that for two weeks, he could take me out every single night.

Dinner, laser tag, pottery painting, cooking class, couples' yoga, trivia night. We did it all, complete with hand holding and making out and everything twelve-year-old Sandra ever dreamed of.

Tonight, he's driven me all the way to Oklahoma City, to a fancy restaurant at the top of Oklahoma's one and only skyscraper. He looks devastatingly handsome in his fitted black suit and new light teal tie. I wear a short, sparkly dress, per Jonny's request.

Dinner is fun but tense. I anticipate that tonight is somehow a replacement or reenactment of the night we almost made love, the night Jonny shattered my emotions into a million incomprehensible pieces.

I am understandably nervous.

I suspect that Jonny is, too, due to his excessive sweating.

We climb into his truck after a delicious meal.

"I want to show you something before we head back," Jonny says as he starts the truck. His voice sounds strange. I take his hand and nod, needing to feel his calloused fingers around mine. I'm intrigued and confused when we pass by my campus. I wonder if he wants to stop at a fountain or in one of the pretty green spaces, but he keeps driving. A couple minutes later, we pull into the driveway of a small house.

"Are we meeting people?" I ask.

He scoffs with a smile. "Like I'd spring that on you. No. Sit tight." He climbs out and pulls out his phone, I assume texting someone inside, because all the lights in and on the home flicker on. He opens my door and helps me out.

Jonny tucks me into his side and turns us to face the house. "It's a cute little place, isn't it?"

"It is," I say, taking in the craftsman exterior that's newly updated, with white paint and black shutters. Thick cedar beams frame the cute porch that's surrounded in bright Morning Glories. A million of them, all blooming and colorful. It makes me smile.

Jonny moves us to walk up toward the front steps. "It needs some more work, but the location is perfect. It'll only take you a few minutes to get to a lecture or the hospital."

"Wait, what?"

"Look, Sand, it was a risk, I'll admit it, but I found it months ago, and I just jumped on it before the price went up. Even though you weren't talking to me, I convinced myself I needed a place in the city and then maybe, on the off-chance you forgave me, if I could fix things, we'd have a place." I am only able to stare at him. "So yes! Yes, I bought you a house. I bought us a house, okay? I told you, you make me crazy! Before you tell me this is irrational or too much or whatever else you're thinking, let's just go look inside, okay?"

I don't answer, but I let him guide me into the house. It's beautiful. It's small but completely updated from top to bottom, with an open entry, kitchen, living and dining room. It has no furniture yet, and some of the light fixtures are missing. It has huge windows on all the exterior walls that still have stickers on them. In fact, it still smells like fresh paint.

"Half the renovations were started when I bought it, then I had some of our contractors finish it out. Two bedrooms, this guest room or office here, hall bath." He leads me through the hall. "Then this is the master."

What? The room is fully decorated?

It's beautiful, like a magazine. Like Jonny's house. There's a king-size bed with fluffy white linens, nightstands, a dresser, built-in shelves with knickknacks and books, there's a rug and a fireplace and—

Our photo on the nightstand. But it's not?

Or it is the same frame from Jonny's house, but not the same photo. I walk over to pick it up. It's a similar shot; Jonny's in a football uniform but in high school. He towers over me and has his arm around me almost as if trying to lock my head in a choke hold. But I'm not just gazing up at him in this shot; instead, we're looking at each other, laughing.

"That was my first varsity game. Do you remember? Rob didn't even bother coming, but there you were, next to my parents, looking at me like I was an NFL MVP. Made me so amped I think I played my one of my best games ever that night."

"I do remember."

Jonny walks over to me and takes the frame out of my hand and reaches behind me to put it back on the table. We're chest to chest like we've been a million times these past two weeks, but it's different this time. My entire epidermis reacts to Jonny's closeness. Jonny puts his hands on my waist.

"You can redecorate in here however you want, but just know, in a couple months when you're getting the swing of your third-year schedule, I'm gonna propose." I hear myself gasp, and Jonny looks down to my lips with a devious smile, then back to my eyes. "Yup, then we're gonna get married pretty quick. Whatever kind of wedding you want, big or small, wherever, whatever you dreamed up when we were young. I'll pay for it because I know your parents are gonna be touchy about the whole thing. So keep in mind, I'm moving in here relatively soon, and I'm gonna make a mess of the closet and leave my toothbrush on the counter and all kinds of things that will make you crazy." His right hand moves from my waist around to my backside, and he squeezes me, so hard I whimper. Jonny licks his lips and then whispers as he pulls me closer to him. "You good with all that so far?"

I nod.

"Tell me, Sandy. Tell me if you want that or not."

"Yesss, I want thhhhat."

Jonny's big teal irises light up. "Good. I thought we could stay here tonight, hence the furniture. And I brought some of our stuff." I try to nod, but Jonny keeps rubbing and squeezing me with his right hand as he talks. "I thought we could christen the place—is that stupid?"

"No." Did I manage to say that out loud? I did!

Jonny scoops me up and lays me down on the bed, then stands back.

"You mean so much to me, it hurts to look at you sometimes, here, in my chest." He places a hand on his sternum under his tie, then he starts to unbutton his shirt. "And you're so hot, Sandy. The sexy way you're looking at me right now, I've thought about this every day since that night." He keeps his eyes on mine as he gets completely naked, and I watch, in awe. I'm still completely dressed.

Jonny takes off my sandals, and kisses each of my ankles, and then kisses up my calves and thighs, which are exposed in my short dress. He lifts up and hovers his whole body over mine.

"Now I want to kiss you where you've never been kissed, and you're going to freak out at first. Do you trust me?" I nod, and he smiles before kissing me, hard. His tongue explores my whole mouth before he nips at my lip and moans. As he kisses my neck, he works my underwear off and out from under me. He moves back to push up my dress. His mouth goes back to my inner thigh, as his hands lock with both of mine. His mouth…

His…

I…

"Relax, Sweetheart. Focus on how good it feels."

O…

K…

Wait…

Wow…

Wowowowowowow…

…

…

"Jonny!"

He holds me up as I shudder and then collapse. He kisses my neck, saying words as he does. He pulls back to look in my eyes.

"Sandy," he whispers. I guess I am able to hear and process sounds again. "Can I take your dress off? I want to see you." I nod, and he works my dress off my body. He sits back on his haunches, still fully naked and apparently fully aroused. "Wow. Again. Still. Always." He reaches down to kiss my abdomen, stomach, up to my breasts, neck, then back down and back up, over and over. Licking and kissing and sucking and I think biting? It's the best feeling I've ever felt, but it's not enough.

"Jonny, I want to touch you."

"Yes, ma'am," he whispers, then guides my hand to him. He keeps his hand on mine and teaches me how to move. Jonny closes his eyes and stills my hand. "Let me get protection."

"I'm on thhhhe pill."

He lines himself up and then leans over and kisses me. "Are you sure, Sandy? I can wait."

"P-p-positive."

"I'm nervous, too, sweetheart." He pushes my sweaty hair back from my forehead. "I love you. I'm in love with you. You know that, right?"

I nod and smile and squeeze my eyes shut because tears are trying to come out. Jonny rubs his nose along mine. "You can cry, Sandy, as long as you promise me they're happy tears."

"They are," I say just as one escapes.

"Open your eyes, Sandygirl. Watch me make love to you," he whispers. I open my eyes to see teal, bright, brilliant teal, before he thrusts into me and—

He...

I...

Him...

Jonny...

Me...

Us.

EPILOGUE

Many Years Later

My senses are exhausted and overloaded, but still, I hear him in the hall. "I'm here! I'm here, Sandygirl! Sweetheart! I made it!"

Jonny bursts into the room as if he owns the whole building, as if he owns the whole city. He's also smiling as if he is not, in fact, in very deep shit with his wife. Peak Jonny.

"You're a d-d-d-"

"Dead man. I know, Sweetheart, I know. I did fly private to get back, but there was a small problem with the plane."

"WHAT!" I cannot afford to tense up right now. And this is not a good time in my career to commit murder and suffer a trial, jail time, etcetera.

"But I'm here. Let's do this."

My doctor ignores my husband. "Dr. Canton, it's time to push now. You know the drill."

I do.

I push and groan and scream and try to let my body do what it wants to do. And I try my best to break Jonny's hand.

Twenty long minutes later, she's here.

"It's a girl! Hot damn, I have five baby girls!" Jonny yells, well beyond what the acceptable volume for a hospital room. But just as he has at the last four births, when he cuts the umbilical cord and places our daughter on my chest, he can't speak at all.

I...

She...

Our newborn baby.

She's perfect.

"She looks like a Sally to me," Jonny whispers.

"Ann-n-n-other S name? Isn't that too much?"

"I'd name them all Sandra Junior if it were up to me." His beautiful eyes look from me to, apparently, Sally. He whispers, "You hear that, baby girl? You grow up to be a beautiful genius, just like your mama."

Tears fall faster now. Jonny's big warm hands wipe them away before he leans in to kiss my forehead.

"I love you so much," he croaks out.

I try to talk, but it comes out a happy sob "I lllll—"

"I know you do, sweetheart." His eyes fill so full I think he might actually cry this time. "I can't believe I got so lucky. You love me better than anyone has ever loved anybody. You always have."

IF YOU ENJOYED THIS BOOK

Thanks so much for reading! If you enjoyed reading *Things I Always Wanted*, please consider leaving a review on your platform of choice. For indie authors, the most important things in life are coffee and book reviews. Okay, I'm mostly kidding. But if you have a minute, leaving a rating or review will help me find more awesome readers like you.

THE HEARTLANDER SERIES

I hope you enjoyed this short novel as an introduction to the Canton family! Want more Heartlanders? Read the swoony love stories of each of Jonny and Sandra's five daughters—Susan, Sadie, Skye, Samantha, and Sally. Each installment is smart, steamy, full length, and complete with surprise twists, laugh-out-loud banter, a happily ever after, and a sisters group text thread you'll wish you could join.

Things I Should've Said, An introvert/extrovert romantic comedy
Read a sample: kelseyhumphreys.com/thingsishouldhavesaid

Things I Overshared, An extrovert/introvert romantic comedy
Read a sample: kelseyhumphreys.com/thingsiovershared

Things I Remember

Things I Forgot

Things I'd Never Do

...and maybe more.

Look for all the Heartlanders Series news, playlists,

lookbooks and more at

kelseyhumphreys.com/heartlanders

MORE FREE BOOKS

Get advanced copies of my all my romantic comedies" for FREE by joining my Launch Squad! Sign up at *kelseyhumphreys.com/launch*

WRITERS GONNA READ

I read about a book every two days. Yes, really. So if you'd like my monthly

book recommendations, join my book club! Sign up at

kelseyhumphreys.com/bookclub

ABOUT KELSEY HUMPHREYS

After tens of millions of video views, comedian Kelsey Humphreys has captured her hilarious, heart-warming characters in book form. Her steamy stories dig into deep truths about love, identity, purpose, and family. When she's not writing romance or creating comedy videos, she is reading, running, momming and wife-ing in Oklahoma.

She also writes fantasy and paranormal romance under the pen name K.A. Humphreys.

Follow her funny posts on Facebook, Instagram, and TikTok @TheKelseyHumphreys.

CPSIA information can be obtained
at www.ICGtesting.com
Printed in the USA
LVHW092321250723
753490LV00031B/554

9 781959 428015